Remember Me

**Center Point
Large Print**

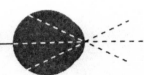

**This Large Print Book carries the
Seal of Approval of N.A.V.H.**

Remember Me

DEBORAH BEDFORD

CENTER POINT PUBLISHING
THORNDIKE, MAINE

This Center Point Large Print edition
is published in the year 2006 by arrangement with
Warner Faith, a division of the Time Warner Book Group.

The text of this Large Print edition is unabridged. In other
aspects, this book may vary from the original edition.
Printed in the United States of America.
Set in 16-point Times New Roman type.

ISBN 1-58547-761-3

Library of Congress Cataloging-in-Publication Data

Bedford, Deborah.
    Remember me / Deborah Bedford.--Center Point large print ed.
        p. cm.
    ISBN 1-58547-761-3 (lib. bdg. : alk. paper)
        1. Clergy--Fiction. 2. Faith--Fiction. 3. Large type books. I. Title.

PS3602.E34R46 2006
813'.6--dc22

                                                              2005034313

To those who have struggled to let go.

Remember the former things, those of long ago;
I am God, and there is no other;
I am God, and there is none like me.
I make known the end from the beginning,
From ancient times, what is still to come.
I say: My purpose will stand,
And I will do all that I please.

ISAIAH 47:9–10

ACKNOWLEDGMENTS

To the four pastors who will always be a part of our lives: Dr. John Ogden, who married us; Pastor Jim Clark, who was there when the babies were born; Pastor Paul Hayden, who is so much fun to hang out with on the sidelines; and Pastor Mike Atkins, who will always be a friend of the dearest kind. We treasure you and thank God for you every day.

To Terri Hayden and Micah Atkins, who were willing to tell stories.

To Alfred P. Gibbs, whose article "The Preacher's Call" proved helpful in my personal life as well as in this novel.

To the women who have stood beside me in prayer with every book and have continued in faithfulness during this one: Patty Atkins, Louise Kiessling, Pam Micca, Luann Wilkinson, Natalie Stewart, Michele Hall, Loleen Denney, Kate Halsey, Theresa Hunger, Cindy Cruse, Sharon Putz, Pat Markell, Maria Lennon, and Jackie Lance.

To my friend Sherrie Lord, who generously offered her insights about military children and how it feels to parent them.

To my talented editor at Warner Faith, Leslie Peterson, and to my agent and friend, Kathryn Helmers.

To Tinsley Spessard, who rounded out this novel with her study questions; and to Louisa Myrin, who dotted every *i* and crossed every *t*.

To my children: Jeff, who is off to the big world of Arizona State University, and Avery, who got her braces off yesterday. I look at you both and I am so proud of you that I ache.

To Jack, my helpmate, primary chauffeur, cook, fisherman, performer at campfires, body surfer in Mexico, and feeder of the dogs while I am writing. Here's to plenty of nights together in front of the fire this winter.

Finally, to Mother and Daddy, who *are* each other's first loves, who celebrated their golden wedding anniversary during the writing of *Remember Me*. There is no greater gift children can have than what you have given all of us. And, to think! You were only seventeen.

D.B.

PART ONE

The Beginning

CHAPTER ONE

Sam takes the steps to the house two at a time, stumbling over the soles of his size-13 tire-tread sandals. For one moment he stands there, breathing in the moldering smell of the porch, the glass door panels clouded with salt and grime, the doorknob scored with rust, the shingles paint chipped, gray or green or white. He can't remember what color they used to be.

He takes one deep, satisfied breath and knocks. He knows exactly what he is going to say. He's been driving for more than two days to see her, across the broad nothingness of Wyoming, the width of lower Idaho, the high plains plateau of eastern Oregon and finally along a snaking, fast highway—terrifying because of the semis—before plummeting toward the sea. When he bangs on the door again, the rusty doorframe rattles and the curtain wavers in cadence with his fist. "Aubrey! I'm here! Hey!"

It seems odd that the dog hasn't started yipping inside. Mox, the McCarts' black-and-white mutt, is always the first to greet him, nails clicking as he charges across the slippery hardwood floor. Then, only seconds after the dog, Aubrey will come, too, shoving

11

aside the curtain to see who is outside, yanking open the door and grinning at him. Her feet will be squeezed into pumps with pointed toes and her pale eyes, which he knows she wears heavily lined so she'll resemble Priscilla Presley, will narrow with pleasure.

Sam, she will say, did you know that a duck's quack doesn't echo and no one knows why?

He will box at her with his hands and say, "I never fall for your silly stories anymore. You know that about me. You might as well quit trying."

When he tries the doorbell, he finds it's disconnected. He jiggles the doorknob, listens for sounds inside the house. He bangs again, harder this time, so hard that it hurts his knuckles.

The sound of his banging fades away and the out-door sounds grow loud. Breeze rattles the myrtlewood leaves. Two flies dive bomb each other beside his ear. The Douglas fir beside the curb seems to watch him, limbs skirting its trunk like a southern belle's gown.

Sam leans toward the glass, tries to peer through it, uses his sleeve to wipe off the murk. "Aubrey?"

When he straightens, someone is standing on the porch next door. A neighbor, he thinks her name is Mrs. Branton, examines him through pinched, suspicious eyes.

"What you want over there, boy? What's all the noise about?"

He's still so surprised to find no one at home at the McCarts', he just stares dumbly.

"You're disturbing people's peace. Do you know

12

that? I'll bet they can hear that pounding for ten miles around."

"Didn't mean to bother anybody."

"Well, you are. You young people, wrapped up in your own vim and vigor. Always thinking about yourselves."

Sam feels his face flush with embarrassment.

"I've got a cake in the oven over here. You keep knocking like that, you're going to make it fall."

"I'm sorry," he says. Then, "Do you know where they are?"

"Who?"

"The McCarts."

"Oh, good heavens. You're not looking for them, are you?"

He nods.

"Nobody's coming to that door, young man. They aren't there anymore."

"Aubrey? Mr. McCart? Mox?"

"Oh, that Mox. Always digging in my garden. No, he's gone, too."

Sam doesn't know what to say.

"Didn't even take time to sell the house. They left too fast for that. Up and walked out, all in a day."

"Do you know where? Why?"

"Packed the car and locked the door. That's all anybody knows. Nobody's seen them since."

"But the boats—"

"Sold to another company. Some Portland people not interested in fishing. They painted the wharf, spiffed it

*up. Now they have box lunches, take people out looking
for whales."*

*From where he stands, Sam sees driftwood over-
grown with dunegrass and wild Oregon roses. He sees
the long smudge of beach and the water shimmering at
him, razors of silver almost burning his eyes. Somewhere near the rocks, farther out than he can see, he
knows there are sea lions basking in the sun.*

*"I suppose you're like those other boys. Everybody
around here was sweet on Aubrey."*

*Her words pelt him like stones, fall off, do not seem
real. He turns from Mrs. Branton, aimlessly tries the
doorknob again and thinks,* I am not sweet on her, no.
It's much more than that. *Then he thinks,* Lord, I
thought you intended us to know each other a long
time. How could you let it end this way?

When Sam Tibbits was young, he'd found it impossible
to think about anything else as long as the sea was
breaking over the shore at his toes and the tide was running swiftly upriver. The ocean had the power to drown
out the news of helicopters crashing in Vietnam, or
thoughts of the *Ed Sullivan Show*—which he would be
missing because the motor court where they were
staying didn't have a television set—or even thoughts
of the skateboard his father had promised him if he
mowed Madelyn Vance's yard all summer.

He had wanted to pretend that he belonged here year-
round, that he wasn't a city visitor always doomed to
depart after a week's rental. He wanted to know the

times of the tides and the diesel smells of boats and the sorts of bait that might coax things onto his hook and out of the water.

Something in him awakened every time he came to Piddock Beach. He wanted to be a boy of the sea.

From the moment seven years ago, when his father had first parked their new two-door Plymouth Fury at Sunset Vue Motor Court and Sam had launched himself forward, folding his mother halfway into her seat as he grappled for the door handle, he had been desperate to get to the water.

"Hold your horses, young man! The beach isn't going anywhere in the next five minutes." But his mother reached for the latch anyway to let him escape and his seven-year-old sister, Brenda, tumbled out behind him.

"Can I get the shovel out of the trunk?"

His father climbed out and headed toward the neon-lit registration office. "I'm going to check us into the room first, son."

"But it'll be dark soon. I won't be able to dig anything if I can't see."

"This isn't going to take but a minute."

"Dad, we've been in the car for three *days*." They had been stuffed inside the Plymouth for what seemed like forever, listening to the radio cross-country and peeling Saran Wrap off of sandwiches that smelled of ripe, warm ham.

But Edward Tibbits kept walking.

"You never know!" Sam insisted to his father's squared shoulders. "I might be able to dig up some clams before supper, if you let me go now."

Edward turned. For five, ten seconds, Sam watched his father weighing a decision that Sam was too young to understand. Looking back, he recognized what it was—the first hint of his father relaxing in months as he breathed in sodden, salt-ridden air, his face losing its tight, hard edges. But he felt it at some deeper level, and it became another reason that the boy loved the sea.

With a slight, knowing smile, his father tossed the Fury keys toward him. "Time's a'wasting, isn't it, boy? Get your shovel."

"Yeah." Sam snagged the keys in mid-air.

A long list of commands from his mother followed: "You watch your sister, Sam. Don't get too close to the water. Remember that you have to wear those pants all week; don't mess them up now." Her voice might as well have sailed off into the wind. Sam got his shovel and sprinted toward the sand, down a row of rickety steps, glancing back with irritation at his annoying little sister who was hurrying after him. Brenda clung to the railing, climbing down the weatherworn stairs. Her sandals slapped the wood.

"You're going too *fast*," she complained. He could see her getting teary-eyed. "You're supposed to watch out for me. Mom said."

"You don't have to hold on, Brenda. Just *run*. Come *on*."

By the time she caught up, he was sitting in a clump of dunegrass tearing off his sneakers. He left his two socks in knots on the sand, brandished the shovel and raced toward the waves.

"I have to take my shoes off, Sam. Wait for me!"

The sun had begun to sink, silvering the water that skimmed the shore. A gathering of plovers strutted on toothpick legs, the birds' phantom strides pressing the sand dry in tiny spots. Ah! Sam grinned. Cold, wet beach beneath his bare feet! There was nothing in the world that could make him wait for this.

"There's splinters in my hand. See the splinters? Can't you get them out?" Brenda shoved her small grimy hand toward his face.

"Just *deal with it,* Brenda."

Another wave rushed toward them and, as it subsided, bubbles emerged from the earth around him. Once, Sam might have thought these marked the residences of clams. Now he knew better. He had made a friend at the school library, Mr. Crisp, who had shown him pictures in books and told him not to look for holes, but for churning indentations, signs of the clams burrowing in the shallow water along the seashore.

Sam set out in search of those kind of marks, completely ignoring his sister. He spied a promising place and began to dig. He speared the sand with his shovel and turned over a pile of it, sorting through it with his fingers, certain he'd found something for supper.

But, no. Nothing.

He tried another spot while Brenda traipsed behind him, her shoes squishing because she'd never had the time to take them off, her splintery hand still upraised, her fingers curling out like a starfish. "Sammy Tibbits.

If you don't take care of me, Mom is going to *bust* your *bottom*."

Sam rolled his eyes and continued to explore and dig in the shallows for at least another quarter mile before he finally stuck the shovel into the ground and stared at the ruddy Oregon sunset in disappointment. He'd been so certain he would find clams.

At that moment Sam noticed the girl standing out where the waves crashed and rolled over the end of the jetty.

Her silhouette against the darkening sky made the girl's knobby-kneed legs looked as stilt-like as a sandpiper's. He couldn't help but stare. She stared back as if she were examining Sam for some purpose, as if she knew already that her presence in his life would be a certain thing.

"Sammy," Brenda whined. "I'm gonna tell!"

"Okay," Sam said, turning to his sister. "Dad has tweezers in the car box. We'll go back and have Dad take care of your hand."

The girl began bounding toward them, leaping with no effort from rock to rock, her yellow culottes flagging in the wind. As she jumped forward, he saw that she was shouting at him. Spray pounded the jetty. She approached him without hesitating, hopping down off the rocks, so confident that you'd have thought she owned the whole of Tillamook County.

"You won't get anything if you keep digging like that."

"Oh, no?"

"Nope. Not at all." The gap between her front teeth made her smile interesting. Her eyes reflected the waves, a clear coke-bottle green.

"This is how everybody says I should do it."

"Everybody *says*." He could see where she had swiped her cheek and left sand there. Salt air matted her brown hair. Even her bangs were sticky, poking from her forehead in the same shape as a crab's claw. "But nobody must have ever *shown* you."

"There aren't any clams on this beach anyway."

"You don't think so?"

"No."

She dragged a piece of hair out of her eyes. "Look," she said, taking his shovel from him. "I'll show you clams."

He followed after the girl with Brenda in tow, as the girl sifted through the shallows with dirty, bare feet. Just when Sam least expected it, she speared the ground and began to scoop three times as fast as he could have ever done it, siphoning off shovelfuls of liquid sand with easy, economic tosses of the spade.

"No clams on this beach, huh?" she asked as she pulled one out and handed it to him. Then she found another. And another. And although Sam could have been perturbed because he hadn't been the one to actually haul these out of the ground, his enthusiasm overshadowed his pique. He had now *seen* seafood come out of the ground! These were the biggest, fattest, roundest clams! Sam had expected small ones, the kind he had seen in Howard's Surf and Turf Restaurant, bite-sized morsels steamed and served with melted butter.

"Do you want to take these? Hold out your shirt." The girl offered them to Brenda. "Do you want more than that? Those aren't enough to feed anybody."

Brenda gazed up at her with undisguised awe. "We need a whole bunch."

The jetty girl stayed with them until dusk, digging and pitching clams into the sling of Brenda's shirt. "You ought to take some of these, too," Sam said, trying to be polite.

"I can't," she said, brushing her windblown hair from her face. "I bring home too many. My father told me that I couldn't do it anymore." She pointed to a light that had just appeared on the western horizon, maybe still a half mile out at sea. "You see that?"

"Yeah."

"I'd better go. That's my father's boat. He's coming home."

Sam retrieved his shovel.

"How long you going to be here?"

"A week."

"Longer than some."

Only after she headed off did he realize that he had never asked her name. The girl's footprints pressed deep in the sand until they grew shallow and faint where she had started running.

When Sam and Brenda appeared on the stoop of Room 3 at the Sunset Vue Motor Court, his mother opened the door and gasped. Edward shook his head with pride.

"Well, I guess we did the right thing, letting you run off the way we did, boy. Look what he's done, Terrie! He's gone out and brought back supper just the way he said he would."

"Edward, bring them a towel or something, would you? Don't you two come in here without wiping off. Oh, Brenda, just look at you! You've ruined your shirt."

"I'll go to the front office right now and borrow a pot," their father blustered. "We don't have anything big enough to cook this huge catch."

Beneath his breath, Sam whispered to his sister, "Don't tell."

"I won't," she whispered back.

CHAPTER TWO

Gulls hung in the air the next morning like kites moored to the wharf with string when his father took him to sign up for a deep-sea fishing trip. Occasionally a gull would land on the weathered sign that read, "McCart's Bait Shop," folding its wings against its sides, surveying the fish scales on the pier with interested, yellow eyes.

"No sense taking up room on the boat for me," Sam's mother had told them as she'd scoured the pot a second time this morning before she returned it to the office. "I'd just feel sick, and worry that Brenda might fall over the side."

"We're on vacation for family togetherness, Terrie. This is something we *do* once a year."

"I don't like to watch things get reeled in, gasping until they die. They're so pitiful! I'd much rather take Brenda shopping on the Strand for back-to-school clothes."

"Talk about gasping and dying," Sam's father said.

So there they were, just the two of them, making reservations for a boat.

His father pushed the bait-shop door open and Sam thought that the place smelled even fishier on the inside than it did on the outside. Chicken-wire crab pots dangled overhead. Behind the counter stood three faded, dusty framed photographs of fishing boats—the *Westerly*, the *Stately Mary*, and the *No Nonsense*. His father gestured toward the photos. "You got room for two more on one of those vessels tomorrow?" he asked.

The fellow who stood behind the cash register looked as distinguished as any fisherman, with a leathered face and whiskers as white as minnow bellies. He reached for a black ledger with rusty rings and curled edges. Inside, on green quadrille paper, the penciled names of what must be customers had been written in a small, square hand.

Edward propped his elbow on the counter. "We'd like a salmon trip, if we could."

The man was dressed in a red-plaid shirt with a green Scottish sweater. A button pinned to his chest read A REEL EXPERT CAN TACKLE ANYTHING. "You're talking salmon, you ought to have real good luck this year. Been a good season all the way around."

Outside, from down the pier, came a scraping sound

and the slapping of ropes. "Arlie," someone shouted. "Get on out here and tie us up."

"That's them coming in now." The man named Arlie slammed the ledger shut and hurried outside, leaving them at the counter.

Sam shrugged. His father gripped his hand. "What do you say? Why don't we see what they've brought in?" They hurried outside and walked the length of the wharf, then found themselves pulling ropes, too, heaving the boat hard against tire bumpers, tying knots around rusty iron moorings. The captain climbed out of the *Westerly*, lifted his hand to assist the ladies in sun hats to disembark, as the men in Bermuda shorts, toting Brownie Starmite cameras, helped themselves. A teenage boy, tan and wiry, opened a metal cooler on board and began pitching the day's catch out onto the dock. This must not have been a salmon trip, Sam surmised, but rather a bottom-fishing trip close to shore. The speckled rust body of a lingcod, the silver ribbon of an eel, and a great assortment of spiny sea bass hit the dock.

"Got two more who want to go out with you tomorrow, McCart. You willing to take a group out to deep water?"

"Don't know as I have enough crew—"

"I can do that trip if you want me to." The girl stepped forward on deck, the poles and fishing lures in her hand jangling like wind chimes. "I'd *like* to do it." And when Sam recognized her, he knew that this day, which he had already suspected would be nice, had just become even more interesting.

He waited to see if she would say something about them meeting last night. He was afraid she might say, "Oh, *you're* the one I had to dig all those clams for." She didn't. She only smiled at Sam and he felt instant gratitude.

The girl with the bottle-green eyes propped two poles inside their metal holders on the railing and leapt ashore. "It doesn't always have to be Kenneth who goes out on the deep-water trips."

"Walt McCart." The captain of the *Westerly*, a man with a rectangular, lined face and sun-faded blue eyes, offered his hand. Stiff points of blanched brown hair poked from beneath his billed cap. He looked just as weathered as the man who had taken their reservation inside the bait shop. The captain gestured to the teen beside him who had been dumping fish, ignoring his daughter. "This is my son, Kenneth. He's going to be running these boats someday."

Although his features seemed somewhat plain, Kenneth stood as straight and tall as a sailboat's mast, his brown hair tousled, his eyes darker than his father's, his teeth as white as the gleaming hull of the boat beside him. "Nice to meet you, sir. Hello, Sam."

"Nice to meet you, Kenneth." Edward extended a hand, too, and they shook.

"Just earned his Eagle, isn't that an honor for a Scout? Just got moved to clean-up hitter in his baseball line-up, too."

McCart announced all those accomplishments before

24

he seemed to notice Sam eyeing the one person who hadn't been introduced, the girl standing at her father's side.

"Oh. And this here's my daughter. Aubrey."

"Aubrey," Sam repeated. "Hello, Aubrey."

"Do you want me to show you how many places there are to hide on a boat?" she asked.

He nodded. "Yeah."

While the two fathers made fishing arrangements in the office and Kenneth hauled off a load of fish to be filleted at the Cannery, the two kids clambered onto the boat. Aubrey showed Sam how the long white plank seats on the ship folded open. Beneath the seats were chambers that held the lifejackets, still damp from passengers this morning.

"Climb in," she said.

"What?"

"If you lie down in here and I cover you up with lifejackets and close the lid, nobody will know you're here."

"You'll sit on the seat," Sam said. "You'll sit there and you'll sit on top of me and you won't let me out."

But she climbed in first. "Cover me up."

"You mean we're *both* hiding in here?"

"Hurry up. Kenneth will be back soon. He washes off the deck and he makes me leave and go home."

"I don't know."

"Are you worried? Look, there's no way you'll get stuck. No way to latch it."

If Sam didn't do it, this would make the second time

he was shown up by this girl. He clambered over the side and into the lifejackets, began piling them on top of himself. As Aubrey lay down, she brought the lid over on top of them.

"Watch your hands," she whispered.

"I can't . . . see . . ."

"You don't have to see anything. You have to listen."

"Aubrey? Are you there?"

"Careful not to breathe too hard. If you do, you might run out of air."

That statement made Sam hold his breath in terror. And sure enough, just as Aubrey had said, the sounds around him seemed to magnify, the *slap slap slap* of the waves against the dock, the melancholy bells from the buoys out in the bay, the jukebox playing "Tom Dooley" by the Kingston Trio in a café on the shore.

"He'll come soon," she whispered.

"Why won't Kenneth let you stay on the boat? When it belongs to your father?"

"Kenneth thinks he's in charge of everything." He felt her hand touch his arm. "Just be still."

At that moment, they heard footsteps on the planking, someone whistling a tune. A water hose slapped the pavement. The faucet squeaked. Then a spray pelted the side of the boat in short, broken sweeps.

They had no way of knowing how much time passed. The water washed over the side of the deck, splattered off the railing, trickled into the bay below them. That, too, seemed to make music. A long, unending song.

At last, when the hose smacked the ground again and

the water changed pitch and the faucet squeaked off, Sam waited for the footsteps to move away. "I haven't run out of air yet, Aubrey."

"You won't."

"You said I would."

"I was just teasing."

He began to push his way up out of the lifejackets.

"No, wait. Stay still. Just a minute longer."

"Why?"

"Don't you feel safe, being here?"

He didn't answer right away. "I hadn't thought about it."

"I always feel safe when they don't know where I am."

"That's crazy, Aubrey."

"Maybe."

"You have a bike? If you do, I can teach you to ride on the curb without falling off."

"Okay."

"At first, it can be scary."

"Did you see the Masterson-Linn Mortuary down the street? You want to know the scariest thing I ever did?"

"Yeah. What?"

"My friends and I snuck in there once and tried out the caskets."

Sam didn't quite know what to say. That topped curb-riding, for sure.

"It was kind of like this."

"I want to get out of here now."

"We wanted to try them out. To see if the expensive

27

ones were more comfortable than the cheap ones."

Another boat must have passed because he heard an engine pulsing and the *Westerly* began swaying with the swells. Diesel exhaust stung Sam's nostrils. The boat began to rock as the biggest waves moved on by.

"Well?" he asked.

"Well, what?"

"Were they?"

"Were they what?"

"More comfortable?"

"They were all the same." She was quiet for a moment and then whispered, "He's gone." As she struggled to sit up, she jostled the lifejackets and he felt her movement all around him. Sam shoved open the wooden seat cover and sunlight blinded them both.

It was the way he would feel every summer during the years he spent with Aubrey, visiting Piddock Beach, as if she poured light into his life and it blinded them both.

Below the wharf, at the base of a rickety ladder that led down to the waterline, a platform floated. Three sea lions slept on it, their hides dry from the sun. Aubrey took a handful of bait fish from her father's cooler and pitched them over the side.

One sea lion awakened and rolled backward into the sea. Another, which had surfaced ten yards beyond, jumped for a fish and upset the platform. They all fell in, barked their complaints while a pelican lifted its bill and waggled its pouch at them, sidestepping the noise.

"Did you know that a rhinoceros horn is made of

compacted hair?" he asked.

"Did you know that a puffer fish can hold its breath for two days?"

"You think you know everything."

"Maybe I do."

They stared each other down in unspoken challenge. Later, when they thought of it, neither could decide who had started the race. They dashed up the pier toward land, laughing, weaving among people, their Keds slapping the wooden planks, leaping over fishing poles and water hoses and ropes in the way. They landed in the sea grass at the end of the dock at the exact same time, in a dead tie, and lifted their faces toward clouds rolling in from the Pacific.

"The least I can do is offer you a piece of cake." Mrs. Branton has on an apron with splashes of cabbage roses that is tied so tightly around her waist her belly folds over it like dough. "Angel food." When she reaches to unknot the strings, Sam sees the small white knobs of her knuckles. "If it didn't fall with this clatter you're making, it ought to be good."

Sam is nineteen and, as long as he stays at Iowa State studying liberal arts, he will not go to Vietnam. He has a job serving food at the student-union cafeteria and, in April, the week before Easter, he was handing a plate of meatloaf and French fries over the counter when something came to his head and his heart, the only way he could describe it was a holy urge, and spoke distinctly inside his head.

You have been chosen by me, Sam Tibbits, to feed the ones I love.

He stood there, with the plate still in hand, staring at a classmate who looked like she'd been studying all night and hadn't changed clothes in three days.

If this is what I think it is, *he'd wondered,* if this is God calling me, then shouldn't I hear something more?

Instead, he heard the clatter of the girl's plate as she set it on her tray, the rattling of silverware, the noisy talk that filled the cafeteria, the next person in line ordering roast chicken with green beans.

This summer his head is filled with questions. He longs to talk to Aubrey and see what she thinks about him going to seminary. He knows, from seeing her every year, that her father has never taken her to church. And her opinion won't amount to much compared to that of Pastor Wiley, the man who had baptized Sam when he'd been nine, who had asked about a thousand questions when he heard the story, who had phoned a colleague at a Bible school in Kansas City and had said, "I have a man sitting across from me who has a holy calling on his life. I would like to recommend him to you with warm-hearted approval and authority."

But Aubrey's opinion has always mattered to him more than he would ever let on. He has to see her. Watch her eyes as she hears the news.

She will laugh when he tells her he thinks he's supposed to be a minister. She will poke him in the ribs when he tells her that the heavenly Father did something inside his heart while he was serving meat loaf.

She will shake her head when he tells her about the check for tuition that came in the mail from someone in Nebraska who he doesn't even know.

If he can convince her to come with him, he's decided, this may be his last trip to the sea.

Mrs. Branton squints at him. "She been writing you letters? Maybe you know something we don't."

"Some. It's been a couple of months, though." He pictures her last letter, the way it arrived in his dorm mailbox with Aubrey's handwriting scribbled out and his mother's scribbled in: *Forward to Madison Hall, Rm. 211, Ames, Iowa.*

"They've been gone almost two months."

Sam tries to remember a date, a postmark, something she wrote that might clue him in. He remembers her last few letters as unsatisfying, too generic, not Aubrey's normal mix of jokes and stories. But, he thinks, she certainly had her reasons for that. Sam sees himself returning the pages to the envelope, using it to bookmark his Psychology text. He had been cramming for midterms.

"I heard from her in early spring," he says. "That's the last time."

"Every window's locked tighter than a drum." Mrs. Branton keeps folding and unfolding the broadcloth apron in her hands. "We couldn't stand it. After three weeks or so, Philip carried the ladder over and climbed up so he could see inside. So odd."

"What's odd?"

"The Lighthouse-Reporter *still unfolded beside Walt*

31

McCart's chair. Mox's food still in the bowl. Aubrey's tea bag left on a saucer. As if she intended on coming right back."

Should he have known by anything in her letters that something was wrong? All this time Sam is struggling with disappointment. Now he gives in to fear, too. "Do you think something could have happened to them? Did anyone phone the police?"

"Of course we did. We all thought of doing so. But we're neighbors, not family. They could have gone anywhere, and we'd be fools saying they were missing."

Sam can only think of going down to sit on the beach. He wants to dig his toes deep into the sand where it is cold and wet. He wants to ask questions of the ocean, watch the cresting waves slam toward him, the blue darken as the clouds roll over the sun.

"Did you talk to Arlie? Do you think he would know anything?"

"Arlie's long gone. Married some woman named Hester. She made him move to Medford when McCart sold the boats."

"It would be worth a try. Even though he's not here, he might know something."

"I saw them get into the car, that's the funny thing. I ought to have thought something of it. McCart had his hand on her arm." *She shows Sam a grip above the elbow, tight around the sleeve, as his heart becomes a fist inside his throat.*

"He did that? Like he was making *her go?*"

"Yes. I'm afraid so."

Sam can smell her cake burning inside. He knows she can smell it, too. But they both stand watching each other a moment more, wondering if either of them could do anything for Aubrey now.

CHAPTER THREE

Each year the Tibbits' vacation ended with the same father-son ritual, Edward and Sam perched on a driftwood log watching the rocks turn to silhouettes against the last ocean sunset, the last golden light spreading its fingers up through the sky. The morning before they drove away, there was always a clap on the back at the marina and a promise from Walt McCart for even better fishing next year. Brenda always begged for another cherry phosphate from the soda fountain before they left town. And Aubrey always came running up the walk with a wadded paper sack, gasping for breath because she'd almost missed them, thrusting it toward him and saying, "Here's this year's present to remember me by."

"What is it?"

"You have to look inside and see."

Each year Sam would unfasten the bag and find some treasure. One year it was something hard and poky. He pulled out the inflated carcass of a puffer fish, its dried spines protruding in every direction. Two fake eyes, moving disks of white and black, had been glued in the sockets.

"Let me guess," he said. "It died holding its breath."

"Just shut up."

"Did you know that a dragonfly lives its entire life in two days? In the same amount of time a puffer fish can hold its breath?"

"Write me," she said, as she did every year.

"I will."

"You promise?"

"Yeah. I promise."

And with that, the Tibbits started off on their long drive home to Iowa, Sam waving even after he couldn't see Aubrey anymore. By the time they reached the state line, he was thinking of everything that lay ahead of him instead of everything that lay behind. The grass in Madelyn Vance's yard, *groan.* Swimming in the Cottonwood pool. His baseball team.

Maybe his team would do okay in regionals this year; this suddenly seemed more important than anything. Sam loved hanging out with his teammates in the dugout, ramming his bat against the corrugated roof whenever anyone got a hit. He loved stepping inside the batter's box, lifting his elbow, chewing his bottom lip while he glared at the pitcher.

Sam hadn't thought much about girls before now. There were a few of them his friends liked to tease by stealing their books or slamming shut their locker doors. But roving the school halls in one huge pack and discussing Coach Pearson's outlook on the preseason Minnesota Vikings or the St. Louis Rams seemed more important than anything to do with females. Camping in Big Bluestem Park and watching plastic forks melt

and curl in the fire seemed more intriguing than anything to do with the girls they teased. So Sam kept stories of Aubrey to himself. For some reason, his thoughts
of her felt safer there. Aubrey became a part of him that
he carried within him, but did not share.

Sometimes at sundown, or so Aubrey told Sam and
Brenda one August, in a flash, in an instant, you might
see phosphorescence in the water. For one moment, if
you were watching, the sea glowed green. That same
summer Aubrey proclaimed herself a George Harrison
girl, with shiny posters taped to her walls, a collection
of George buttons lining her bulletin board, and Beatles
albums stacked a foot high beside her record player.

"You should like Paul," Brenda told her. "He's much
cuter."

"I don't see what girls think is so great about the Beatles," Sam said, feeling illogically jealous, unable to
adjust to the sight of the monstrous George face staring
pensively at them from Aubrey's ceiling.

"Will you show the green glow to us?" Brenda asked.

"You want to see it? Okay, but if I try, you have to
promise to look hard. If you blink, you might miss it."

When the three went out, they took the puppy along.
Walt McCart had found Mox curled in the ropes on the
No Nonsense one morning. He said they would never
know whether someone tried to drown the dog or
whether someone just dropped him off at the wharf.
The puppy flopped along with the three of them, a
sand-matted tussle of fur, his hind legs occasionally

overrunning his front ones. People who would not smile at anything would smile at Mox.

"Look at my lips, you two," Brenda said, skipping along beside them.

Sam did his best to ignore her.

"Sam, you have to *look*."

He rolled his eyes. He didn't need to see this. He'd been with her when she'd blown her allowance this morning on the edible wax lips at the Seaside Salt Water Taffy Shoppe on the boardwalk.

"Want some?" Brenda held the bag toward Aubrey.

"Sure."

"You want some lips, Sam?"

"No."

"I think you *do*."

"I don't like chewing wax."

"I think you want *Aubrey's* lips."

He stopped in his tracks, mortified. "Shut up, Brenda. Just shut up."

But it wasn't the first time the thought had come to *his* mind, either.

Aubrey came to the rescue, changing the subject. "You have to hear about the latest thing Kenneth did." Although if Sam hadn't been so desperate to be rescued just then, he might have rolled his eyes at Kenneth stories, too. The last time they'd been deep-sea fishing, McCart had almost missed a thirty-pound Chinook because he'd been busy singing the praises of his son.

Sam steeled himself to hear another story about the "All State Running Back 1963" certificate Kenneth had been awarded last fall, or about the 4-H rosette he'd won for woodworking at the Tillamook County Fair, or about the way Kenneth brought in a record number of fish when he'd captained the *Westerly* and a group of nine Japanese tourists. The more Sam spent time with Aubrey, the more he realized Kenneth McCart was the favorite son of Piddock, Oregon. But, instead she said, "He saved someone's life this spring. Since I last wrote to you."

Sam opened his mouth to say something, and shut it immediately.

"Really?" Brenda stopped in her tracks, too. "Who did he save?"

"A man staying out by the creek."

Sam picked up a shell, ran his thumb over the ridges, pitched it away. Mox bounded after it.

"There was a homeless man who stopped by the wharf when Kenneth was washing down the *Stately Mary*. He asked my brother if he could spare an extra fish. Kenneth asked where he was staying and the man said he had a camp tent set up beside Elbow Creek, just beneath the bridge."

Mox chased after the waves then darted back as they chased him, trying to get to the shell Sam had thrown. Sam looked around for a stick to throw the dog, something that would float. Brenda stood gaping up at Aubrey, listening to the story she was telling.

"They talked about the Alaska earthquake on the news that night. But no one understood what it would do to the sea. And that night, as Kenneth lay in bed listening, he realized he couldn't hear waves anymore. It was what Kenneth *didn't* hear that confused him."

"I don't believe he saved anybody's life." Sam dusted the sand off a piece of driftwood. He lobbed it into the air. The stick boomeranged end over end as Mox scrambled after it. "Kenneth does a lot of things, but I don't believe he did that."

"When you're used to living beside the ocean, when you're used to hearing the constant roar, it is the silence that attracts your attention."

Mox overran the stick and doubled back, looking for it.

"Kenneth said he knew the water had gone out and that it would come rushing in again. He knew the water would flow upstream and flood Elbow Creek. No one except him knew that a homeless man was sleeping up there."

"Wow," Brenda said.

"So he woke Dad and they drove up there. Did you know that? He only had to say the word and my father went with him. My dad never listens to me like that."

Mox had returned without the driftwood. "Someone needs to teach this dog to fetch."

"They got there in time. My brother was pulling him to safety and all around them, the noise started, the sound of the sea wall crumbling, a bridge folding, people shouting from their beds, a log being driven through the side of a car."

Kenneth, the golden child to everyone. "How do you think that would feel?" Sam asked. "Knowing that someone was alive because of you?"

"My father tacked the article up on the wall at the marina beside all the others," Aubrey told them.

LOCAL HERO SAVES A LIFE, the headline in the *Lighthouse-Reporter* read when Sam saw it the next day. The paper ran the story with a picture of Kenneth and a drenched stranger, the canvas tent bubbling up out of the water like a squid. The article related how the teen had scrambled down the underpinnings of the bridge, reached for the man's hand on the rocks where he'd been stranded, while his father held his legs to steady him, and Kenneth dragged the stranger to safety. The water had come from Prince William Sound, the newspaper reported, after the Alaskan earthquake the day before. The remains of the tent hung snagged beneath the span of Elbow Bridge for two more weeks before anyone could bring it down.

"Aubrey?" Brenda asked, and Sam saw his sister's tentative fingers touch Aubrey's. "I don't want to miss the light in the water. Are you watching?"

"I'm always watching."

Sam wasn't sure just why he grasped Aubrey's hand and pulled her along as if he wanted to pull her away from something. Perhaps it was because every time he heard another story about Kenneth, he saw how she lived in her brother's shadow, and sensed she was hurt.

The tide was dead low. The waves broke lightly, far out. Mox followed them to the standing rock that, any other time of day, would be off shore. Around it, gulls were wheeling over the open ground, preying on exposed sea creatures.

Sam let go of Aubrey's hand and lifted Brenda onto the rock. His sister struggled for a foothold. When she finally stood, she lifted her face toward the sky and stretched her arms wide and shrieked, "I'm flying out here. I can fly forever!"

Mox was next to be hoisted up and then Sam gave Aubrey a boost, too, before he scrambled onto the rock beside her. Aubrey pulled her blowing hair into a pony tail. She held it there with her hand because she had no clasp.

"Let's stay here all night," Brenda said, with her face into the wind.

The three of them roosted there, their silhouettes as spindly as cranes against the sky, as the mist drew closer to shore and the distance between their perch and the point of land that marked the downtown marina seemed to grow farther away. The sound of the sea became something beyond them, so loud that they couldn't hear it anymore. The ocean never betrayed her mysterious green light, but one by one, the stars sprang alive overhead.

They stayed so long that Sam thought Brenda might have gone to sleep, leaning against him. He whispered to Aubrey, "I wish I never had to leave."

"This rock?"

"No. Your town."

"I know."

"I'll always come back, you know that? I'll never stay away."

"And I'll always be here."

"That's good."

"Yes," she said. "Good."

When Mox fell, he hit water. They'd been so deep in their reverie, they hadn't realized the tide was coming in. They heard the sound of scrabbling claws, the little yelp, the skittering pebbles, as the puppy struggled. Sam leapt off and found himself knee deep in the dark ocean as the next wave sent up a spray. Aubrey was already in front of him, clapping her hands, bending low, searching.

What a relief when they caught a glimpse of Mox paddling toward shore! Seawater slapped at their legs and, moments later, tugged at their ankles. The ocean rose, fell, broke, rose, fell, broke, as if it didn't know whether to push them toward shore or to tug them out deep. As they washed up on the dune, Sam said, "This is why I believe in God, Aubrey. Because things turn out okay."

She scooped up Mox, a bundle of wet fur, into her arms. She stepped ahead and turned, walking backward. It wasn't easy going; she stumbled over shells and stones that the sea had cast at her feet. "I don't."

"You don't what?"

"Believe in God."

"Why not?"

"I believe in the sea," she said. "It's always there. It isn't like God. You always know what it's going to do."

She tripped over something, maybe a hole in the sand or the remnants of someone's sandcastle, and stumbled

41

again. She landed *oomph,* flat on her rear. Unable to halt his forward progress, Sam landed almost on top of her as Mox yelped and struggled to get out from between them. Sam saved the day by bracing himself with his arms.

"Hi," he said, grinning down at her and the dog.

"Hi."

The power of suggestion, Brenda talking earlier about Aubrey's lips. Here she was on the sand, ripples of surf foaming around her shoulders as she looked up at him, her hair plastered against her face like strands of seaweed. Mox wiggled away and shook himself, spraying both their faces. She shook her head, laughing. Light from the windows in the houses on the cliff above reflected in her eyes.

Aubrey stopped laughing when he lowered his mouth to hers.

Her mouth opened at his slight touch. On her lips, he tasted salt. *Oh, yes.* He knew now that he had imagined it this way, had thought about kissing her more often than he cared to admit. He could feel her breath, could smell her Beeman's gum.

A wave lapped over their legs but neither of them noticed. In the back of his mind, he thought he ought to check on Brenda. When they'd rescued the dog, they'd left his sister alone on the outcropping, watching the sea.

"Why'd you do that?" Aubrey asked.

"Because."

"Because why?"

"Because I wanted to."

Against his T-shirt, Sam's pulse rattled in counter-point to hers. He felt her small breasts pressing against his chest.

"Why did you want to?"

"I don't know."

Breaking waves drummed in the distance. Finally she asked, "We wouldn't want anyone to think we liked each other, would we?"

"No," he said with great certainty, shaking his head.

"Or that we were boyfriend and girlfriend or any-thing."

"No, we wouldn't."

"Because we're *friends*." But her voice sounded stu-pefied, as if she needed to convince herself that the words were true.

"Yes."

Lanterns swayed in the distance on a Coast Guard cutter patrolling the shore. On the far horizon, the last remaining light smudged the line between earth and sky. A buoy bell rang out past Lex's Landing.

"Sam?"

He didn't answer.

"Why so quiet? Didn't you like kissing me?"

Silence.

"You're shaking. Are you scared of me?"

Sam shook his head no, said yes.

She rose to her knees and he arose with her, cradling her neck with his hand, his fingers shoving her hair from her ear. *I'll show you who's scared.* He kissed her again, and Sam felt her hands fall to his shoulders. He felt goose bumps rise on her arms, heard the small sound at the back of her throat. He wasn't shaking anymore.

Somewhere over the roar of the surf he heard a plaintive voice calling him. "Sam?"

The sound didn't register at first.

"*Sam?* Are you *there?*"

They scrambled up, stepping away from each other.

"*Sam?* Are you *coming* to get me?"

He turned to Aubrey. "It's Brenda." Sam trudged into the waves again, sloshing toward the rock. He held up his arms toward his sister.

"I thought you'd forgotten me."

"I wouldn't do that. Come on down now." Brenda slid toward him and Sam broke her descent with his arms. "You want to walk to shore yourself, or you want me to carry you?" But she was ahead of him, already blundering toward shore.

When they arrived on dry ground, Aubrey was waiting for them with her arms wrapped around herself, her palms sliding up and down against her goose bumps. "I have to get to the dock. I promised my father I'd go by the marina tonight and restock the bait cooler."

Sam didn't want her to leave them. He stepped forward, wiped the wet legs of his jeans as if he could dry them. "You have to go?"

"Kenneth's shirts need washing, too."

"How come you have to do house chores and your brother doesn't?"

"He takes care of the boats."

"But *you* want to do that."

Suddenly Mox was upon them again, leaping in the air and shaking and spreading sand. When Sam tried to grab him, he ran in widening, playful circles, just out of reach. "Aubrey, couldn't you stay longer tonight? You could do those things later, couldn't you?"

"I'll get grounded." She clapped her hands to attract the puppy. Mox came to her without hesitating. "Let's go, Mox."

It occurred to Sam that, as long as he knew Aubrey, he would watch her walk away across the sand. And that night in the confines of the motor court, Sam couldn't sleep. On the opposite side of the narrow room from his snoring father, his mother sighing in her sleep, Sam laid awake, awash in this new sensation of kissing someone. His expectant heart throbbed with uncertainty. The ache inside him felt as big and uncomfortable as hunger.

CHAPTER FOUR

A day came during Sam's sixteenth summer when the *Westerly*, the *Stately Mary*, and the *No Nonsense* did not leave their moorings in the afternoon. Sam, who had gone looking for his father, stood hidden at dock's edge and saw it all—Walt McCart's stern jaw, the desperate set of his shoulders.

"Why didn't you tell me before now, Kenneth?" McCart shook a fistful of papers at his son. "I would have done everything I could to talk you out of it."

"I know that. That's why I did it without you."

"You have everything you want waiting here for you. The family business. Your reputation. Why would you need anything else?"

"I'm bigger than this town, Dad. I've outgrown it."

"You're young. Don't you understand that you can't ever outgrow the place that you come from?"

Kenneth opened the ice bin and began pitching fish out, unloading the morning's catch. "There's nothing else I can be taught here. I've seen everything this town has to show me. There is more to life than Piddock Beach and Tillamook County."

His father began pitching fish out too, right beside him. "Foolhardy." A nice-sized Kokanee slapped the floor and slid, shimmered opalescent in the sun. "That's what you are, boy. Just plain foolhardy."

"You saw Bailey Phelps when he came home from basic training this spring. Bailey, who ran his Impala through a fence and got arrested for throwing beer cans off the water tower and was never able to make a curfew?" Kenneth hauled out fish with righteous vigor. They sailed past and landed in a sliding heap— a Chinook salmon, another Kokanee. "You saw him in uniform, snapping a salute to George Bauer. You saw him walking down the street with his chin up and his shoulders back, as if he was ready to face a dragon and win."

"Is this what it's all about, then? You can't stand to let somebody else be a hero? It always has to be you?"

46

"Self-respect, that's what Bailey has now. You could see it in his steps. He's come home a different man."

"I'm proud of you, son. Is that what you need to know?" McCart wiped his forehead with the back of his sleeve. "You don't have to do anything else to make me feel that way."

"This isn't about you, Dad. It's about me. Maybe I love this country so much that I want to fight for it. Did you ever think of that?"

"Yes. A man always thinks of those things."

Their unloading was done. They stood shoulder to shoulder, staring at the heaps of ice in the bin, their muscles taunt, their chests heaving. "I don't mind taking the responsibility. I don't mind standing for a just cause."

"You'll go to Vietnam."

"I will. And I'll come home a man. You remember the stories Grandpa used to tell about his days in France."

"Grandpa's war stories. Your mother would let him talk until we were bleary-eyed and then she'd smile and distract him with blackberry pie."

"I don't mind being a part of what he talked about. I don't mind being a part of something bigger than myself."

In the distance, Sam could hear a radio playing "A Hard Day's Night." The Beatles were everywhere, Sam noted with annoyance.

"You've already enlisted? Is there anything that could still stop you from this?"

"No."

"I could discuss it with your recruiter. Tell him you did this without my permission."

"I'm legally responsible for myself, Dad. I didn't need your permission. What's done is done."

McCart's fists hung like knots at his sides.

"Unless they say I'm not good enough. Unless I don't make the grade. And with me there isn't much chance of that."

"I don't get what you're thinking, risking your life."

Kenneth shrugged.

"If it was college you wanted, I could have sold one of the boats. I would have been able to swing educating my own son." A new effort. Sam could tell Walt McCart was struggling. "That's why I bought the *Westerly* in the first place, so I'd have enough to pass off to you when the time came. So we'd have plenty of vessels to do this together."

"It's too late to have this conversation, Dad."

"You could have seen the world that way."

"I'll get the GI Bill when I come home. This is what I want to do."

McCart ran his hands beneath the water hose. He dried them on an oily rag. "Your mother—"

They were coming close to him. Sam ducked behind a tangle of nets. Kenneth was poised to jump from boat to pier, but he turned back. "What about her?"

"Your mother would say I was wrong for wanting to stop you."

Kenneth lifted his chin. "I wish she was here, then."

McCart gripped the iron railing on the boat. "I've

48

already lost her, son. I didn't intend to lose you, too."

Sam had never thought of Walt McCart as old. Now Sam suddenly saw him that way. When the conversation ended, Kenneth strolled away, walking tall, his heels slapping the wooden planks with purpose. And behind him McCart stared, stoop shouldered, at the tangle of fishing poles and lures and lines as if he had never seen such things before.

Kenneth's going-away party was a major event, with the fried halibut, the cobs of golden Oregon-grown corn, and sliced beefsteak tomatoes as big around as tea saucers. A bonfire cast shifting shadows on the beach. There was picture-taking and hand-shaking and well-wishing. In hours, just after sunrise, Kenneth would catch the Trailways bus and ride to his pre-induction physical in Portland.

Finally, after Kenneth's buddies had drifted to sleep against rocks by the bonfire coals, and families wrapped in blankets strolled toward shore to watch the moon-silvered sea, Sam noticed Aubrey and Kenneth leaning against a sand dune, their voices murmuring.

"You going to be okay, kid?" the brother asked.

"Guess so," the sister answered. "Guess I don't have any other choice."

Even Sam could feel the gulf between them before Kenneth put his hand on her shoulder. "I'm going to miss all those questions you used to ask me, you know that?"

Aubrey was hugging her knees. She lifted her chin

49

from them to talk. "I used to drive you nuts, didn't I?"

"What do you mean *used to?* You still do."

"Shut up, Ken."

" 'How do salmon find their own stream when they spawn?' you'd ask. 'Why doesn't a boy ever ask me to dance?' 'If God made the world, then who made God?' "

Her chin settled against her knees again. "If Mother had been here—"

"I know." Then, "I wish you had known her, Aub. I don't remember much but it was all good."

"I thought so."

For a long time neither spoke, and there was only the sound of the waves sliding in, the whistle of the night birds swooping through the air. "Dad'll come around someday, Aub. He'll see what he's doing and he'll stop thinking I'm the only kid he ever had."

"You think so?"

"Yeah."

"Tell me that's not the reason you're going away. Tell me you're not doing this to give me a chance with him."

"I'm not, sweetie. There's lots more to it than that."

"You really want to do this, don't you?"

"I know you can run those boats. You can take tourists out and do all the things I've been doing. He'll see."

It was the first time Sam had ever seen Aubrey cry. She swiped her nose with the back of her wrist. "I don't want you to go."

"You be careful with boys. I won't be around for awhile to protect you."

"I will."

"There's not a one of them in this town I think is good enough for you."

A sad little laugh. "I'm glad you'll be gone then."

"Hush up, Aubrey. You know what I mean."

"Yeah, I know what you mean."

"You're my sister."

"Yeah."

"I may be leaving now but I'll be back. If anybody's done anything to you that I don't like, I'll whale into them when I come stateside again. You can tell them that."

"Okay."

As Sam watched, he saw Kenneth draw his Swiss Army knife from his shirt pocket, rubbing its red surface to a gleam with his thumb. "Here. You take this."

"Why? So I can protect myself against all these boys you're worrying about?"

"Every girl needs a pocket knife. I'd like for you to have mine."

"That's the one Grandpa gave you for Christmas."

"Yep. Sure is."

When he dropped the tiny red knife in her hand, she stared at it in wonder.

"You don't have to give me this."

"Don't have to." He stood up and stretched. "But I want to."

Her fingers closed around it. Sam had never seen

Aubrey hold anything so tight.

"Now, I've got to get back to the house for a few minutes, throw a few more things in my bag."

"I love you, Kenneth."

"Meet you at the bus stop in a little while, okay?"

To Sam, it seemed like almost no time at all before the crowd at the bus stop grew to include almost the entire town. All to say good-bye to Kenneth. "You go, boy," Arlie said when the red-and-silver Continental Trailways arrived just past sunup, its brakes hissing and its accordion door folding open. "You go show the rest of the world what a Tillamook County kid is made of. You go off and make us proud, you hear?"

"Here here," someone shouted as Kenneth hefted his monstrous duffel. "You keep a hat on during basic," someone else bellowed. "Your head's sure going to get cold without that hair." A roar went up; everyone was calling for him to take care and to write and to tell folks to come try their hand at fishing here. Sam wondered if he was the only one to see it, how Kenneth propped his foot on the first step of the bus, and ignoring what everyone was saying, looked around to find his father.

Walt McCart wasn't there.

"Hey, girl." Kenneth's voice went rough when he finally noticed his sister. Aubrey launched herself at him and he flung his arms around her. He buried his face in her hair and squeezed so hard that her feet came up off the ground. "You remember everything I told you."

52

She nodded.

"You take care of everybody here, okay?"

"I will."

"I'll be home before Christmas."

"I'll make him—" And for a moment Sam thought she was going to say *I'll make him accept this.* But she said instead, "I'll make him shoot us a duck for Christmas dinner."

"Maybe I'll be the one to do the shooting by then."

"I don't want to think about that."

"Hey, boy," the driver growled. "You going to get on this bus any time today? I got two dozen people in here with nothing to do but wait for you."

Kenneth swung himself up and the door folded shut behind him. As the early morning light rippled off the steel and the glass of the bus, all Sam and Aubrey could see was a reflection of each other on the panels of the bus. Then it choked, roared to life, began rolling, disappeared along the highway.

CHAPTER FIVE

February 1968
Dear Sam,

You should read the stories my brother writes to us. I miss him! He's sleeping in Vietnam, he said sometimes better than he slept here, which is a surprise to me. He said they killed pigs in a village and found a house with women and small children but no one else. Then at night there are shadows everywhere and bullets that zing through the air at their feet. He met up with Bailey Phelps and they talked about sophomore English at RBHS, isn't that weird, all the way around the world? Then, that next day, Bailey stepped on a booby trap and got shrapnel in both legs. "This is to confirm that your son was admitted to the Station Hospital in Danang," the telegram said when his parents got it. "Your anxiety is realized and you are reassured that he is receiving the best of care." They are saying that Bailey will get to come home. His mother is happy he got hurt so then he can be okay. Isn't that the oddest thing, when you think about it? Wanting something to get hurt so it can be brought back to you in the end?

Love, your friend, Aubrey

May 1968
Dear Sam,

I can understand how everybody where you are is talking about Vietnam. Did they really say that about our soldiers decimating villages where innocent people live? I think about the women and children being the only ones not to hide, the things that Kenneth is writing me, how they wonder if the broad smiles on the women's faces mean one thing or if they mean another. How everything gets spooky at night when the shadows come out and the grass rustles around them and there isn't any way to tell which person is your friend and which is your enemy. You know how Kenneth is. He wouldn't hurt someone out of anger or frustration. But he might make a mistake. It is the people who lose it everyone talks about. The strong ones remain without changing and no one tells stories about them at all.

Your friend forever, Aubrey

October 1968
Dear Sam,

It was so good seeing you. I miss you so much! You complained that I only write about Kenneth and that I never write about myself. So I'll fix that. You asked what I was thinking about going off to college like you. Well, you ought to know the answer to that one! My father was willing to sell a boat to keep Kenneth out of Vietnam, but that wouldn't happen for me! I've got a part-time job this summer waiting tables at the Sea Basket and I've been able to save a little that way. Maybe I'll go to Portland in a year or so. Someday I'd like to be a teacher, did I ever tell you that? First graders or kindergarten, I think, because I want to be a person who teaches children to read. When I got my MIA bracelet, you won't believe this, it's for a boy from close to you! What do you think that means? His name is Private Louis R. Markell from Des Moines. He disappeared when a helicopter went down over Quang Tri.

Love, Aubrey

April 1969
Dear Sam,

Kenneth says that you are definitely right about the mosquitoes. He says the only way he keeps track of weeks going by is that, on Sundays, they give everybody malaria pills. By the way, thank you for saying you are praying for him. I told Dad that, too, and Dad crossed his arms and said "Hummph," and walked away. Kenneth writes that his commander yelled at him for jumping off a blown-up bridge into a river somewhere close to Phu Bon. The steel girders were blown apart and twisted underwater, his commander yelled at him, and he could have impaled himself. But it was worth it all, he wrote, because underwater he found the mark of a clam bed. He snuck to the river later and dug freshwater clams for his buddies. The clams were different from the ones here, no larger than a nickel, but he boiled water in a canteen cup and steamed them and they opened up like the ones here. It's just like Kenneth, don't you think? He could have gotten speared. He could have died. But he managed to find something that made him think of home instead.

Love, Aubrey

October 1969
Dear Sam,

We piece together what we know of the war from Kenneth's letters and what we hear on TV. Sometimes he writes long stories. Other times he writes a few sentences and that is all. Those are the letters that scare me the most, the ones where it sounds like my brother's writing fast or he's afraid to tell us what he has to say. There are more stories on the news about protestors here than there are about the soldiers who are fighting. I watch footage on TV and think maybe I'll see Kenneth sometimes, but you know my father. Whenever the news comes on, he leaves the room.

I think about the times we had such a good time together. Do you remember the night we met and I dug up all those clams and gave them to Brenda? You never told anybody that was me, did you?

Arlie got dragged down to the Oregon State Fair by some lady named Hester who wanted him to ride a roller coaster with her and he threw up. He talks about all the years he rode out the sea, but he couldn't make it on the Wildcat Coaster. He says he's glad anyway. He doesn't want to

57

worry about women. He doesn't think Hester will call him again.

oxoxoxoxox, Aubrey

May 1970
Dear Sam,

I keep thinking about what you said about wishing our country could go back to the way it used to be before the war started. You're right, every day that this moves forward, something happens that makes us not be able to move back again. I think about this a lot. Life changes, that's what makes it dear.

In regard to helping other countries be free, I do know this much. Everybody wants the same thing. It's just that nobody can figure for sure how we ought to get there. So, do you really think Nixon did the wrong thing by invading Cambodia? I know he said that, when he got elected, he'd bring the war to an honorable end. I know we're all waiting for that. When you've got somebody over there that you love every hour is another hour too long. Every hour is a time when something could go wrong.

Another thing about time, I can't believe it's almost *summer*. See you SOON, I hope!!!!

Aubrey

• • •

For all her letters that Sam had practically memorized, he did not remember the specific words she chose to tell him her brother had died. He remembered only the impact of Aubrey's words, the shocking news scribbled on her thin blue stationery. He remembered only his throat closing, his eyes scurrying over the words a second time, incredulous that she chose to relay the details of Kenneth's demise in this spare, dry way.

Her father hadn't received a telegram like the Phelpses. Instead, at ten in the morning, she wrote, the day after New Year's Day, a solitary officer came striding up their walk, dressed in Army green from his head to his ankles. Walt McCart wouldn't answer the door. He made his daughter stand before the man and ask what he wanted with them.

The officer wouldn't talk to me, Aubrey wrote. *All those times my father ran away from watching the news because he didn't want to see it. He could not run away this time.*

"On behalf of the secretary of the Army, I regret to inform you that your son, Private Kenneth Jay McCart, has been killed by enemy fire in Cambodia," the man had said, doffing his beret. "The McCart family has our deepest condolences."

Sam felt cheated because the letter arrived too late for him to come to the funeral. *Why didn't you phone me?* he wanted to ask her. *Why didn't you let me know about Kenneth as soon as it happened?* He would have driven maniacally across five states to reach her. It saddened him that he hadn't been there to stand beside her, to support her with a hand against her spine, bracing her while mourners murmured and filed past, paying last respects to her fallen brother.

Aubrey had never given him the chance.

As Mrs. Branson sets her watering can on the stoop, spins her hanging flower pot and observes it from every side, Sam recalls his last miles driving here along the two-lane from Portland to the coast. With each mile after he turned off the highway this morning, the dense Sitka spruce seemed to grow more impermeable around him. Five miles southwest on the road and he could still see the sun. But somewhere along there, the Douglas fir and towering hemlock began to thread their limbs together like woven fingers overhead.

For a while he could still see patches of blue. Then that, too, had disappeared even though it was not yet midday.

When he'd been little and they'd stopped because he had to pee, his mother had followed him along the rest-stop path. She said she was afraid she might lose him here, that the foliage was growing so thick that she might never see him again. He'd been disappointed, of course. Being a ten-year-old boy, he hadn't intended to actually use the men's room. He'd wanted to hold onto the raggedy moss-covered trunk of a monstrous tree and inspect the ivy and blackberries and vincas growing in the ground, where before he'd only seen such things growing in the garden center at Hy-Vee.

He'd wanted to listen to moisture dripping from a fern. He'd wanted to pretend he was an explorer like Lewis and Clark, traipsing through a primeval forest that no one had ever seen.

The mossy darkness, the feeling of being hemmed in, the skewed sense of distance, had suited him perfectly this morning as he drove here. Sam kept thinking his Mustang's odometer was off. Every time it read that he'd gone a mile, he was sure he'd gone three instead. The narrow hands in his chrome dashboard clock seemed to rocket forward at an impossible pace.

He'd started practicing the words while he traversed the rolling hills and cornfields of his home state. He had become more certain of them as he'd passed waves of grass in Nebraska, oceans of sagebrush and herds of antelope in the Rocky Mountain West. "We're young, Aubrey," he planned to say with his entire soul. "Hasn't losing Kenneth made you see that you were right? When you wrote to me how life changes? I'm not willing to risk what we have together by staying on some yearly vacation schedule where I always end up telling you good-bye." Then Sam would say, "I'm asking you to marry me, Aubrey. That's why I've come."

He'd been picturing her staring at him in disbelief, arguing against it. But Sam wouldn't listen because he had heroism on his side. He was young and, like most young people, he knew that his way was the only fitting way. He intended to rescue her. Although he knew the hardest part of this for her would be to leave the sea.

The logistics had come shooting at him at the same speed as the white lines in the center of the coastal road. "You could come to Iowa with me," he would say. "We could live with my parents while I go to seminary; I know it would be all right."

Then his car had broken out of the shore pines and onto the tidelands and the sky suddenly sailed above him. He saw hedges of salal and fragrant wild roses and dunegrass where the earth gave way to the beach. The bright shavings on the water blinded him. He had to squint and fumble for his Ray-Bans before he could make his turn. And he'd driven directly to the McCart's house, screeched to a halt beside the dented mailbox at the curb. When he'd taken the stairs two at a time and banged on the door loud enough to bring out the neighbor, he'd known that his life had been about to change. Until Mrs. Branton came out to meet him, Sam hadn't imagined it changing this different way.

Mrs. Branton uses her fingernails to pinch off dead fuchsia blooms that look like hanging lanterns. She sorts systematically through the leaves. "You haven't been around this place since Kenneth McCart died, have you?" One dead bloom falls to the ground, then another. She says, "This must be hard for you, too."

Watching her pinch flowers does not chase away the images he still fights in his head. The pageantry of a military funeral, a twenty-one-gun salute, a Color Guard, the flag folded into a tight triangle, handed over into defeated hands. He wonders if the casket came from Masterson-Linn, if it could have been one that Aubrey had tried out for comfort.

"You know what people are saying, don't you?" Mrs. Branton asks as she lifts the watering can and a stream runs from its spout into the soil. "They're saying that anyone would do well enough to be rid of that family."

"What are you talking about?"

"Losing a boy like that, when the father didn't want him to go in the first place. They're saying losing Kenneth got to them. They're saying Walt McCart wasn't the same again, that the girl got desperate trying to make him see that he had another child besides the son he'd lost. They say she decided she couldn't ever be good enough for her father so she went the other way."

"I don't understand."

"Maybe that's why the house looks like somebody's coming back. When Aubrey left, maybe she didn't know that she wouldn't be back again. They're saying McCart had to do something fast because that girl got herself into trouble."

"Trouble?"

"Yes. You know. Trouble. The family way."

"Not Aubrey. I don't think so." But maybe, he reminds himself, he doesn't really know.

Oh, Father. What do you want me to do now?

Sam pictures the fishing nets and the crab pots at the deserted bait shop swaying overhead. He hears Walt McCart's voice asking his boy, "Is this what you wanted, Kenneth? This is the self respect you wanted? Well, you got it now. See?"

Sam feels as if he has reached for something flashing past him and has just barely missed it.

The only person he knows to call is Brenda. She is a young woman now, too, and often very wise. When he tells his sister why he had come all this way and what he was thinking, she tells him what he needs to hear.

"That beach town was never your real life, Sam," she tells him. "That place isn't about reality; it isn't what it's made out to be. Come home, Sam. You're crazy if you don't give this up."

"What about Aubrey?"

"What about her?"

"I'm in love with her."

"Give yourself more benefit than that, Sam. You're in love with a time and a place. You're in love with the dream of Aubrey. She was never a part of who you are here."

"But knowing Aubrey is here makes me be *the person that I am there."*

"Mom and Dad will say the same thing. I'm sorry that you're hurt, but you have your whole life in front of you."

"I know."

"You already know that God has something special for you in mind."

"Yes," he says quietly, "but I thought Aubrey was going to be a part of that."

"I think you ought to come home."

Late in the evening, before he leaves, Sam walks

64

alone beside the waving dunegrass. He climbs over driftwood. Shells shatter beneath his feet. He shoves his hands inside his pockets, jiggles his coins and the Mustang keys. He stands still and gazes into the distance, his heart a flood tide of regret, as he looks over the dark horizon of the sea.

PART TWO
Present Day

CHAPTER SIX

The ancient Volkswagen van pulled next to the curb, parked, and sat in the dark outside the house on Burn Hill Lane. After a good amount of time passed, almost twenty minutes or so, he opened the rusty van door, wincing at its groan. The hinges could use a good dose of WD-40, Hunter thought. They had definitely seen better days.

"Over there." He pointed to the dark hulk of a house to their left. "In the garage."

His partner let out a low whistle.

Hunter felt inside his jeans pocket. Yes, the keys were still there. Yes, he admitted, he felt the slightest tinge of guilt for what he was about to do.

But only the slightest tinge.

His father had promised Hunter for years that he would get his uncle to let him drive this car.

When you're old enough, his dad had said, *then I'll ask. When you've practiced and gotten your license and have enough experience to understand what a* real *engine feels like.*

Anyway, a person wasn't actually stealing, Hunter reasoned, if he only planned to borrow something for a while.

Ryan Dowell, Hunter's best friend, led the way across the dark lawn. "I can't believe a pastor would have an old car like this stashed away somewhere." He stood on tiptoe and peered through the grimy glass. He stepped away as Hunter inched the garage door up off the ground.

"It's under a sheet. He keeps it covered."

Ryan whistled again.

"Sh-h-hhh."

Hunter's breath came in shallow bursts, his blood pulsing in his own ears. This low spark of danger pleased him. For the first time in months, Hunter felt alive.

More alive than he had since the day his father checked into the hospital to stay, when Hunter had no words. It had always been a struggle to express his emotions. "Jab," he'd said instead as he squared off like a boxer and gave his dad a light punch on the elbow.

"Jab back," and his father had cuffed him, too.

A boxing match was so much easier than talking. So much easier than watching his father, frail and tired in his hospital bed, stare at his mother as if he needed to memorize something he might never see again.

When Hunter opened the garage door, a dark, hollow room, smelling of dust and lawn fertilizer and gasoline, loomed ahead of them. Reaching up, he dared to grab hold of the old light chain and a bare bulb came to life. He whipped the sheet off with the same finesse a magician would use to whip a tablecloth from beneath a load of china. The sheet billowed into the air for a moment before it fell into a pool at his feet.

"Wow."

"I know."

Ryan ran his fingers along the red surface. "This is something."

"A 1965 Mustang Coupe. Everything's original. Even the seats."

"He hasn't redone anything?"

"He bought it used when he was in high school. He's kept it this way ever since."

Ryan ran a hand over the black leather headrest. "I'll bet she really cooks."

"A 289 V-8."

"Not a six-cylinder?"

"No. This one's a hot ride, man." Hunter pitched Ryan the keys. "He won't know anything's been touched. He checks the tires ever so often. Makes sure the battery's good. Other than that, he hasn't taken it out for years." Hunter's words were more for himself than his friend.

Ryan steered and Hunter pushed. When the Mustang began to creep into the open night air, its wheels crunched over pebbles. That was the only sound. By the time they were at the end of the driveway, their hair was wet and they were sweating because of the heat. The car jostled into the dip at the curb and Ryan steered it into the road.

Two houses down, Hunter motioned for Ryan to take the passenger side. He climbed in himself and started the motor. They skulked to the end of the block in the dark, the motor pulsing beneath their seats like something alive.

Hunter fumbled with a knob on the dashboard when they reached a cul-de-sac. The high beams came on. The blank façade of a house in front of them, the grassy lawn, the pavement, were all flooded with light. Hunter would have to choose whether to go left or right. He chose left. "You ready? You want to see what she'll do?"

Ryan nodded and Hunter stomped the gas.

Tires squealed and they started pulling G's. They careened around the curve, topped out at the corner of Toboggan Drive. Hunter took a wide left onto Toboggan, which led them toward Main Street.

He whipped the wheel to the left when they pulled up behind a pickup truck. They swerved into the oncoming lane. "This baby's got burners."

"We goin' through the center of town?"

Hunter downshifted in answer. In spite of the stifling heat, drops of sweat from his hair chilled his neck.

He would not be able to explain to anyone later why he chose to do it. The thrill of fear, perhaps. Or maybe just lunacy. He loved the way it felt to control the car, to control *something*. At the yellow traffic light on Main Street, Hunter reached for the knob, cut the headlights, and boomeranged into the intersection as the light turned red. Ryan's head crashed against the window.

"You're killing me."

Hunter downshifted again, accelerated.

Ryan reached behind his shoulder for the seatbelt and didn't find one.

"It's on the seat, man. No shoulder harnesses back in the old days."

Ryan fumbled behind his hip and found the belt. He shoved it into the metal buckle with a fleeting sense of relief. "Cut it out, Hunter. You don't have to prove anything to me."

Hunter's lunatic momentum wouldn't let him stop. Danger, who cared! He *felt* something. The fear in him proved that he hadn't died, too. He sped through the four-way stop in the darkness, crouching forward, gripping the wheel as if that would let him hold onto everything that had been stolen from *him*. Ahead, in the next block, a car began to pull out, its yellow headlights streaming low, crosshatching the pavement. Hunter whipped the wheel to the right and they roared around it.

They crossed a deserted bridge, the guard rail flickering past like frames in a film reel. A yellow Iowa highway sign loomed and was gone; they'd left the streetlamps of town well behind. They crested hills, veered around turns, hit open corn country driving blind.

A midsummer moon suddenly soared above the ridge as Hunter took every curve by instinct. For a moment the bright orb in the sky made Hunter squint. His eyes adjusted to the silvery path of moonlight and he floored the pedal again, ripping through the intersection at Brodick Lane.

He had no idea why a truck would be parked on the shoulder. If he had been flying with his lights, he would have seen the extra banks of reflectors overhead, the trailer's broad back gate that read "Corn-Fed Beef from the Richness of the Heartland. Atkins Approved!" If he had been flying with lights, he would have been visible as he topped the hill, and the driver would have waved one of the flares he was hurriedly setting.

Three head of Angus cattle, corn-fed and hefty, were roving along the roadbed. The driver, who had stopped to examine a blown tire, had opened the gate to check the stock, never thinking that the angry blast and the flying rubber and the wobbling trailer would incite a stampede. He'd very nearly been trampled as the cows rushed into the road.

When the Mustang shot past in nothing more than a stunning whir, the driver waved his arms to warn them, but it was too dark.

Hunter slowed a bit as he buzzed past the trailer. The smell of manure made him wince. Too late, he saw the massive animal loom in front of him.

Ryan cursed. Hunter plastered his brakes. The tires

screeched. A flare lit the night. The whites of the cow's eyes shone, rolled back into its head with fear.

On impact, everything went blank.

CHAPTER SEVEN

The wedding reception took place on the lawn of a turn-of-the-century house in the Sherman Hill Historic District, three blocks away from the church. Pastor Samuel James Tibbits, who made a point to appear at the party when he had been the one to conduct the ceremony, balanced his plate of Swedish meatballs while he stabbed a small square of exotic cheese with a toothpick. Beyond the wedding cake, red punch flowed from a gleaming silver fountain, making the same noise as a pump on a fish aquarium.

Ah, love, Sam thought as he stood beside candles in iron stands that were impaled into the lawn like tribal weapons. *All is white lace now, but these youngsters have a lot ahead of them.*

"Hey, Sam. Great ceremony for the kids. Thank you." Grant Ransom extended a hand across the chafing dish.

Sam shook the man's hand soundly. Grant had been a confidant, a deacon and a member of Covenant Heights Community Church for many years. Over time the two men had shared worship, prayer, and the sometimes muddy depths of each other's souls.

Grant clapped him on the back. "It wouldn't have been the same if you hadn't done the service. You know how much you mean to all of us, Sam."

"It means a lot to me, too, Grant. Besides, being a part of weddings is one of my favorite things to do."

The deacon gave his pastor a knowing look. "Better than the funeral you had to do last week." The deacon's voice had suddenly gone somber. "Poor Joe. Such a tragedy."

"Yes. It was."

The somberness stretched between them. The yard grew noisy with the clicking of cicadas, so much louder than the wedding guests surrounding them. Sam could still hardly believe he'd lost his good friend and brother-in-law. For one beat, two, he couldn't breathe in the sweltering heat.

Grant brought them back to the wedding. "Simon's a good man for Laura, I think. I *hope*. You know how it is, never easy to give up a daughter."

Sam speared a meatball. "No, I don't imagine it would be."

"All those years of ballet recitals and boys' pictures torn from magazines and those rubber elastics from her braces everywhere."

"You've always made it sound like so much fun."

"It *was* fun. Except for the bongo lessons. The only thing that wasn't fun was the bongo lessons."

"Now somebody else gets to worry about all that. Maybe she'll take up the bongos again—in her own home."

"I knew you'd do that, Sam. I knew you'd make me see the good side."

Sam returned the clap on his friend's back. "Laura's a

beautiful bride. You did a good job, Dad."

After Grant left, Sam deposited his plate with a fellow who came by with a tray. He chose to remain a few moments longer, surveying the fairy-tale setting from beside a ficus tree, not knowing why he wasn't able to touch the joy and the *hope* of his ministry anymore.

Of all places a pastor ought to feel expectant and glad, it ought to be at a wedding.

This morning he had spent an hour poring over financial statements because the re-siding project at Covenant Heights had cost more than the original bid. He had spent an hour in a rousing debate with Lester Kraft about cosmology and the age of the earth. The entire time which he kept thinking, *If I could learn all these scientific threads fast enough, I could argue intelligently. But I don't have time to learn it all!* He had spent an hour with Dottie Graham who had received a telegram that her son had been injured in an Army maneuver and who had been unable to talk to him by phone.

"We'll trust that the money for the siding will come from somewhere," he'd said in a phone message to the chairman of his finance committee.

"Give me a week to do research on the carbon-dating of the rocks in Tanzania," he'd said to Lester, "but in the meantime, I stick by my theological point of view."

"God may not have caused this accident to happen," he said to Dottie as she plucked tissues from the box he held in his hand, "but you must remember that all things work for the good of those who love the Lord.

You must remember that, although you can't nurse your son back to health right now, the Father can."

He knew he was off the mark for thinking it, but he couldn't stop himself. *Father, I know I'm wrong but, ever since Joe died, I feel like I'm covering for you!*

The wedding ceremony had been beautiful, but Sam felt weary to the marrow of his bones. He cast his eyes toward the stars as he shrugged off his jacket, tossed it across the front seat of his car, and loosened his tie. His stomach growled as he drove off, but that didn't concern him much.

He had found certain benefits in being a single pastor. If you counted his one childhood romance with Aubrey McCart, you could say that he'd almost made it to the altar twice. He'd dated during seminary, thinking it important to find a woman who would stand beside him to serve his church. But the women he met there each had their own callings upon their lives. He'd been serious about one woman there, but she'd headed to the missionary field in Indonesia.

Perhaps the closest he had ever come to asking another woman to marry him had been Elaine Ferguson, a young divorcee who had come to him for counseling. Elaine had twin sons, age eight, who she protected from knowing that she was going out to dinner and for walks in the park with the pastor. The more Sam watched Elaine's heart open before the Father, the more he realized that she could be the partner he'd been waiting for. But the more she accepted God's healing in her life, the more she began to realize that she still loved the father of her sons. That had been another beautiful wedding ceremony Sam had performed, the remarriage of Elaine Ferguson to her ex-husband.

Long ago, Sam had decided that perhaps the Father meant for him to serve the church without a woman beside him.

Well-meaning churchgoers were always phoning to tell him about the perfect lady, someone they had met on a plane or in line at the checkout counter at the market or at Edie's Cut 'n' Curl having a perm. Once he'd taken Mary Grace Pokorny out for a quiet seafood supper and, before they'd even been served their snow crab legs and shrimp scampi, two separate Covenant Heights members had called his cell to inquire about the seriousness of their relationship.

"I'm sorry," he'd mouthed across the table at Mary Grace each time before he'd cupped his hand over the cell phone and said kindly, "I'm tied up at the moment. Can I phone you back?"

Each time Sam shoved his Nokia into his suit jacket, he'd contemplated Mary Grace across the table and wavered between gratefulness and irony. Since the board had hired her as his secretary three years ago, Mary Grace had been the one person at Covenant Heights whom he'd been able to bounce ideas off of and know she'd respond with discretion, acuity, and logic.

Lately, she had agreed to take an issue to her prayer closet that Sam felt was of the utmost importance: a weekly meal for the homeless people who slept in camps or under bridges or in the bus kiosks on Walnut Street. Starting a new project at Covenant Heights might make it necessary to discontinue an old, beloved one. So many in the church wanted to serve the Father, but were fearful of upsetting the status quo. How Sam appreciated Mary Grace seeking wisdom and the Father's will beside him.

The irony of Mary Grace Pokorny was this: Sam not only found her full of zest and dependable; he also found her pretty. She reminded him of some colorful, crested tropic-bird flitting in and out of his office. But Mary Grace was not someone he could get to know with subtlety. One supper with her and his parishioners were already buzzing. Being uncertain, as he was, of the Father's will for his life in this area, Sam decided it would be safer to keep Mary Grace as an employee who offered friendly support, and not pursue anything further. At Covenant Heights, too many people were watching.

The meatballs at the Ransom wedding reception had only whetted Sam's appetite. He planned to select something from his massive assortment of casseroles when he arrived home. He had a freezer full of casseroles. They showed up at the oddest times in the oddest places and, whether they were being delivered out of pity or out of feminine guile, he could never be sure.

Something with macaroni, pepperonis, and Parmesan cheese in Tupperware was found dangling in a plastic bag from his front doorknob. Another, filled with Tater Tots, mushroom soup, and ground beef, complete with warming instructions written on a Post-It note, appeared one morning on his deck railing. An enchilada and black-bean surprise had been positioned strategically beside Sam's computer in the pastor's study. A cheesecake with cherry topping materialized in the third-grade Sunday school room with his name on it. Once, when he'd been in a hurry to take a seat for a staff meeting, he'd almost sat on a spinach quiche.

Truth be told, when Sam rounded the corner and saw the car parked at his curb tonight, he thought it might be someone else sneaking casseroles into place. When his headlights splashed across the license plate, though, he recognized his sister.

"Brenda?" The dome light had come on and she was just climbing out. "What's wrong? Is everything okay? How long have you been here?"

"I'm sorry, Sam. Oh, Sam, I'm so, so sorry."

He could tell that she had been crying. Instinctively, he began to direct her the same way he directed anyone else who might come to him distraught. "Come inside the house, sis. Tell me what's going on."

She was speaking in hiccups. "I, I know you've had a long day. I know you had that, that wedding tonight."

"It's okay."

"I've been waiting for you for an hour."

He always left a lamp on for the dog, but he hit the main switch and the lights came on in the front room. On the entry hall table lay a stack of mail he had dropped without getting a chance to read it. Sections of the latest *USA Today* edition were strewn beside his favorite leather chair. His golden retriever, Ginny, peered up at him from where she overflowed the seat without lifting her head. Her eyes were elongated pools of guilt and her beating tail asked him a question. "Busted, Ginny. Out of the chair, girl. That's not your place."

Reluctantly, Ginny untangled herself and climbed down. Sam dropped his jacket on the table that held coffee mugs from three separate mornings, his reading glasses, and *The Weight of Glory* by C. S. Lewis tented open to the page he'd been reading.

"Another rough one tonight?" He offered Brenda a hug but she didn't step into it. So he offered her a box of tissues instead.

"It isn't Joe. You aren't going to want . . . to want to hug me when you hear what's happened."

"What is it, then? Here. Blow."

She took a Kleenex and blew, made the sound of a small horn. When she raised her eyes to his again, they looked as regretful and guilt-ridden as Ginny had looked in his chair.

"Come on, Brenda. What?"

Brenda fished something from her pocket. She dangled them in the air for a moment before she dropped them on the table beside C. S. Lewis. He stared. It had been so long since he'd actually looked at these that it took him several beats to recognize them.

The pewter key chain in the shape of a gray whale,

the pressed letters that read COME AWAY TO PIDDOCK BEACH.

"Where did those come from?"

"You don't want to know."

"Which means?"

"Which means, they came from Hunter. I got them from Hunter."

For the first time, Sam realized that Brenda's trouble might include him. "How can that be?"

"Some crazy thing, you know." She began to get weepy again. Sam knew he was wrong but he couldn't deny a flicker of impatience. She was taking so *long.* "Joe, Joe must have said once, said that you would let Hunter drive your car. Do you ever, ever remember Joe saying that? Hunter was trying to take his father up on some, some promise maybe—at least that's what he said. But no one understands the rest of it."

Sam clasped her shoulders with both hands. She felt as bony and small and fragile beneath his grasp as a bird. He thought, how could someone so small carry all the things that she is carrying now?

She was still speaking in sharp sobs. "Hunter wrecked, Hunter wrecked your Mustang."

For a moment Sam didn't know what to say. The only escape, to first mumble something unintelligible about the wedding. Then, "Brenda," he managed. "Is he hurt?"

"No. He's not in the hospital like Ryan. He walked away without a scratch."

"Someone else was hurt?"

"Yes, yes. A boy riding with him." Then, "Someone who thought Hunter was his *friend*."

"Hunter wasn't hurt?"

"There was this c-cow that never made it to the meat market."

And so Sam finally understood the extent of it. "My Mustang?"

"Totaled."

Sam made himself ask about the other boy, dimly heard that he was injured but would only need a night in the hospital. But his mind was on the car. Ridiculous that he would feel devastated about the Mustang. How could he, when there had been human lives at stake? But Sam felt the worst kind of violation!

He'd treasured that Mustang since he'd been eighteen and had plunked down every penny he'd made after five years as a paper boy and mowing yards and sacking groceries at Hy-Vee. He'd treasured it since the first night it sat in his own garage, vacuumed and polished, when he'd fallen asleep cradled in the leather seat. He'd awakened to it the next morning the way a child awakes the day after a birthday, having to remind himself that something wonderful had happened, not quite believing the feel of the steering wheel beneath his fingers.

Sam reminded himself that his main concern should be his nephew, Hunter. Hunter, who had always made Sam smile at the bustle and noise that one small boy could create during the day.

He'd watched Brenda hold Hunter's face between her

hands with a love so gentle that it made Sam's heart ache. When Hunter's eyes stopped darting and Sam's sister knew her son was listening, she would tell him something necessary for him to hear. "You need to kiss your grandma thank you for the Christmas gift" or "You need to flush" or "You have to wait for me and hold my hand before we cross the street."

"Having a child is like seeing yourself before you made all your mistakes," Joe had told him once when he and Sam had been standing together, watching Hunter sleep. "It makes you feel like you have the chance to be the same person and a different person all over again."

Sam made himself release his sister's shoulders, knowing full well that he'd been clutching her tight enough to hurt her. She was so small, so frail after everything she'd gone through. He had so many questions and no idea where to begin.

"Seatbelts?"

She nodded.

"So that's why they weren't hurt worse, isn't it?"

"Hunter was playing some ridiculous game . . . game of chicken." Brenda swiped at her tears with the tissue, which had been reduced to a small shredded knot in her fist. "Driving through stop lights without the headlights on. Maybe he thought it was the safest way to steal your car so no one would see him. Maybe he was tempting fate. I don't know. How do I know what he's thinking?"

"He's in jail, isn't he?"

"Overnight, that's all. Only because he couldn't pay the fines. There might be charges of reckless endangerment if Ryan chooses. There are stolen vehicle charges—"

"Brenda."

"—which you may *have* to press if you want your insurance to do anything. I'm so, so sorry."

"Stop saying you're sorry, Brenda. You don't have to apologize for him."

Impossible, Sam kept thinking the whole time she was talking, that something like this could have happened, seconds ticking by, details unfolding, while he'd been standing someplace else not thinking of anything except the bride and groom in front of him. He hadn't felt a sense, not even a *nudge,* that anything might be wrong.

At that moment Sam looked at his sister, really looked at her, and felt overcome by his own selfishness. He'd been dealing with his own emotions when he could see that she was falling apart. The crumpled look of her face nearly did him in. "Doesn't it ever, ever stop, Sam?" she asked him. "This awful *hurting* we're going through?"

"I don't know."

"I try to find the good things about losing Joe, Sam. I really do. The length of time we had to tell him goodbye. The life insurance, how he left us taken care of so well."

She stood with one hand on her heart, as if she were doing penance for the things she could not release. With a palm braced against her spine, he guided her toward the nearest chair.

Brenda lifted her face to him as she sat. "You, you want to know what else is good? I cleaned out his toolbox and took all the screwdrivers to the resale shop. I always told him he had too many screwdrivers."

Sam removed the frayed Kleenex from her grasp. She let him have it without resisting.

"I sleep on one side of the bed until it's dirty, then I sleep on the other side, did you know that? Who would have thought about that? Who would have thought that without Joe I wouldn't be washing the sheets so much?"

Sam would let her keep talking, he knew that much. At times like this, there wasn't anything he could say.

"Did you know I get to drink the milk I want now, too? None of that two percent that I always bought for Joe. Now it's only the good stuff, whole milk. It's like drinking cream. Isn't doing what I want supposed to be a good thing?"

He took her hand again.

"Oh Sam," and she began to sob uncontrollably again. "A boy needs . . . a man when he's this age, and I need a husband. Why would God take him, Sam? Didn't God *know?* Why would he take Joe away from us right when we needed him like this?"

"I don't know, Brenda. I really don't."

"I have no idea what to do with Hunter. He doesn't know how to survive this any more than I do."

Ginny the dog had pressed herself in against Brenda's

hip, sensing distress in her humans. She put her head in Brenda's lap and whined.

"I never intended doing this by myself, Sam."

Sam plucked handfuls of tissues out of the box for her, handing her tufts of them halfway as a joke, trying to cheer her up. He felt physical pain watching his sister grieve.

"I keep thinking that Hunter could have . . . have died, too."

"Yes. Yes, he could have." And beneath it all, the thought of Hunter pushing the limit made Sam furious. *He would have done it to himself,* he wanted to remind his sister. *You would have been hurt again and it would have been your son's own fault.*

CHAPTER EIGHT

Sam kept a fake philodendron in his office because he thought he needed a bit of green. Silk, not fake, as Mary Grace was always reminding him. That never failed to make him laugh.

"Okay, okay," he would tell her. "Silk, it is. Silk is better than dead. Anything trying to grow in here wouldn't survive."

Once or twice a year someone would present Sam with a begonia or an ivy, something potted in actual soil. The gift plant would motivate him to use Miracle Gro, to water and pinch off yellowing leaves the way he'd seen that woman—what was her name—in Oregon. Mrs. Branton. Caring for her hanging baskets.

But time would pass and Sam would always be side-tracked by the people he needed to tend to, and would forget to water any plants. A day would come when he'd realize there weren't more yellow leaves to pick. Nothing was left but a stick. He'd carry the pot to the Dumpster, shaking his head, thinking how something had gotten out of order.

He was much better at caring for people and conducting meetings. Even though the meeting that had adjourned five minutes earlier had not been an easy one. Next year's budget wasn't at all what Sam had requested. The finance committee hadn't cut any from the outreach fund but hadn't voted to add anything, either. Instead, the members had allotted something new to the building-and-grounds fund for lighting the parking lot, when Sam had spoken to them about setting up the sit-down supper for the homeless who roamed the area near Walnut Street instead.

The homeless people were fed every night at the shelter downtown, the deacons had reminded him. But Sam had something different in mind; this was why he had asked Mary Grace to pray over it and give him her opinion. Sam suspected his flock was being called not only to offer food but also to offer friendship. Sam knew how the Father worked; he had seen what his congregation was capable of. He ached for them to discover this about themselves: that they could become a family to those who were most lonely, that they could listen and sympathize and pray, that they could return another week to listen and sympathize and pray more, that they could be privy to miracles, that they could reap blessings and benefits because they, themselves, had stepped forward to be a blessing.

It filled Sam with purpose to see his congregation searching out a new journey.

Beside his desk in the windowsill, Sam kept his *Strong's* dictionary and his Bible concordance, his well-thumbed copy of *Taking on the Gods: The Task of Pastoral Counsel*, and a miniature Eiffel Tower that David and Sue Hawthorne had brought him from their vacation in France. Next to the tower, he'd placed a small plaque that read A FRIEND IS A RARE BOOK OF BUT ONE COPY IS MADE.

Sam's Epiphone guitar stood in the corner. The Mustang he'd kept hidden in his garage and his guitar were his most precious possessions. Whenever the business of running a church overwhelmed him, he'd play a chord on the Epiphone, strum a few bars, hum a few words about the love of the Lord making him whole, and some of the weight would fall away.

Which was exactly what he had been doing *that* day. That terrible day when their lives took such a terrible turn. He remembered it perfectly; he had pushed aside the jumbled pages of the budget and reached for the guitar when Mary Grace had knocked on his door.

He went ahead and strummed a C-chord anyway. "You need me for something?"

She hadn't flitted into his office or draped her wrist across the knob the way she usually did. She hadn't smiled at him or tilted her head or told him she thought he'd done an inspired job on the sermon he'd preached yesterday. Instead, Mary Grace had waited with her hands clasped in front of her, her eyes boring into his.

"What's wrong?"

"I'm afraid I have bad news."

"My mother?" Sam didn't hesitate; his adrenaline was already flowing. He and Brenda had gotten so much bad news about their mother lately. She had fallen at the Living Center. She had survived a bout of the flu.

Mary Grace took a step forward, looked as if she wanted to touch his arm. But she didn't. "No, it isn't your mother. It's your brother-in-law."

"Joe? What's wrong with Joe?"

"He's checked himself into the medical clinic. I would have put him right through to you, but you were counseling Dottie Graham and I knew you wouldn't want to be interrupted."

"What did he say?"

"He needs you. He wants you to talk to his doctor first so you can talk to Brenda. He wants you to come over as soon as you can."

The guitar was forgotten. "Will you call him back? Tell him I'm on my way?"

"Yes, I will."

As Sam ran out past her, he saw Mary Grace was already dialing the phone.

The Central Medical Center's family conference room on the second floor was anything but comfortable and inviting. The gold tweed couch leaned to one side, favoring a broken leg. A bulletin board was still covered with meeting notices, their dates long-since come and gone.

One telephone sat in the middle of the floor, its naked cord snaking toward the wall. Sam stared at Joe's doctor in disbelief. The hum of the air conditioner made Sam feel like he was swimming through a blur.

Babesiosis was what the doctor called it, Sam learned. Joe had not noticed the tick bite for far too long.

"You can take care of that, can't you? I thought these days they could treat tick bites with antibiotics."

"Yes," the doctor said, nodding. "That is something we can try. But antibiotics may not be enough since we didn't catch this when it began."

From that moment on, Sam's call to pray for Joe's recovery became a physical stirring. A trembling along his skin. A moving current that traveled the length of his bones, buzzed his ears, warmed his fingers. *I'll pray, Father,* Sam promised. *I'll fast. I'll do anything you ask. I'll do everything the right way if you'll just keep Joe from dying.*

So, he did. Sam prayed, fasted, read one particular verse from 2 Samuel aloud at least fifty times—the one about God being strength, a shield, a stronghold when David stared death in the face, whenever Brenda called with more discouraging news. Finally, when the doctors ordered Joe moved to critical care, and Sam grew too frustrated to do anything else, he donned his shorts and shoes, and started running.

The trail followed the Des Moines River for miles toward Saylorville Lake and each time he went out he ran like he wanted his feet to punish the pavement. While others walked their dogs or lingered beside daffodils that grew like bright springtime teacups in manicured beds, Sam pounded along, pushing his lungs to the limit, every footfall echoing the cry of his heart.

Please, Lord, not Joe.

Oh please, Lord. Not Joe.

How could he feel so stirred, he wondered, if the heavenly Father hadn't planned to do something profound about his praying?

Sam spent his time at Joe's bedside thinking *No, God. Not this. Not this,* while he tried not to notice that the skin beneath Joe's Iowa State ring had turned pale and translucent, as fragile as parchment, as if he might die.

"You've got to promise me—" Joe struggled weakly to prop himself up on an elbow. "—you won't tell people about after the bachelor party."

"Don't try to talk, bud. You just get better. Save your strength."

"I know you're going to want to tell stories at my service, but I don't want you to tell how you wouldn't leave me by myself that night, and I didn't have money for the taxi so I gave the driver my belt."

"There won't be any service, Joe. You're going to get better, I'm sure of it."

"Brenda can't hear that story about the belt. That belt was real Canadian leather. Brenda picked it out."

"There won't be any stories."

"Well, if Brenda hears that one, she'll kill me."

They both stopped to ponder that, and laughed.

"Remember—" And it was the last time they would laugh together although neither of them knew it. "—how that driver made me take it off so he could measure and see if it fit before he gave us a ride?"

"That was ridiculous, trading your clothes for transportation."

"I didn't see you offering to pay."

"No."

"I would never have acted like such an idiot with somebody who wasn't my best friend."

When the sky is a cloudless larkspur blue on the morning of a funeral, a person can feel like the heavens are mocking him, too, for what he believes. The heat fell so heavy outside that it rippled in the air. As Sam stood in the pulpit at Covenant Heights (his sister had begged him to do the service) with that senseless sunlight streaming in across the crowd, he watched Brenda's hand tracing helpless figure-eights across her son's shoulders.

Sam gripped the sides of the pulpit like the railing of a pitching ship. He controlled his own breath, drawing air into his lungs, slowly letting it out again, because breathing was the only thing that felt real.

Only a smattering of spaces remained in the church, all of them in the front three pews. Mourners were even crowded into the back foyer. They jostled for position in the space beside the sound booth. Standing room only. Joe would have liked that.

After Sam delivered a short eulogy, he began to hand the microphone around. So many raised a hand to speak. So many, trying to make sense of it.

How numb he felt, standing before this flock of believers. Thank heavens he didn't cry. But the feeling of *not* grieving, not *feeling,* was awful, too. He felt as dry and brittle and deserted as a drift log left on the beach by high tide.

The void didn't fool him, though. He had stayed with Brenda and Hunter during the four days after Joe's death. He knew that the emotions would return in vicious gulps and waves, surges that would bowl them all over like a child caught in an undertow.

The morning of the funeral, he'd found Brenda with her nose pressed inside Joe's toilet kit as if she wanted to disappear inside it, to cling to these items that had been touched daily by her husband, his small black comb, his nail clippers, a lip balm still shaped by the curve and lines of his mouth.

"You know what gets me?" Brenda had asked him when he found her. "It isn't Joe's chore lists or his notes to himself I find lying around. It isn't bits of his handwriting I find everywhere. It's thinking that I can tell him things."

They exchanged another hug. There had been so many now that Sam had lost count.

"I forget that he isn't here. I'll be right in the middle of something totally unrelated and thinking, *Oh! Wait until Joe hears about this.* And then I remember that he's gone."

She'd begun crying again, a grieving so personal and primitive—soft helpless moans that struck Sam as too private to be viewed. He wished he could step away. He wished he could grieve for Joe that way, too.

A slide show played on overhead screens at the funeral service now, the same screens where words to praise songs ribboned past on Sundays. Sam watched his congregation's faces and knew what they were watching attentively. He had learned to count on their reactions. He had learned to measure their eyes and see their hearts.

Joe, still a toddler, beside the tree on Christmas morning.

Joe, grinning beside Brenda in her satin bridal gown.

Joe, toting his new baby the same way he'd tote a football, completely enthralled and amused.

Hunter, shrieking with joy while he rode piggyback on his father's shoulders.

Hunter, beaming, holding on to one end of the fish stringer while his dad held on to the other end, five small trout dangling from the chain like charms dangle from a bracelet.

Why didn't you intervene, Lord? Why didn't you change this outcome?

When the service ended at the church, the mourners stepped into the parking lot and released bouquets of silver balloons into the aching blue. Sam watched the balloons longer than others did, yearning to see them go higher. Muted, somber conversations began all around him and still he didn't look away.

He watched until they looked like bubbles in the ocean of sky. Until they caught a high current and moved as one toward the northwest. Until the balloons looked like pinpricks. Until there was nothing more to see.

Sam asked his question to an empty sky.

Why couldn't I summon your power, Lord, when it was my own family that needed it most?

"Come inside, Pastor Tibbits." Dottie Graham swatted at a bee that had been interested in his shoulder. "The women's ministry is serving refreshments."

I know you are the faithful one, Father, so what is it about me *that was wrong?*

"We asked Mary Grace about serving something and she said it would be okay."

Inside, lemonade in a Gatorade dispenser and towers of Dixie cups awaited the parishioners. There were brownies dusted with sugar, oatmeal-raisin cookies, slices of poppy seed bread, a deli tray of cheese. Coffee gurgled out of a gleaming, stainless urn. A portrait of Jesus, faded by the years, looked down on them from the wall.

People who weren't standing close had more ani-mated discussions. The ones who remained nearby tem-pered their voices as they murmured condolences, struggling to say the right thing.

"Good service, Pastor. You did a fine job for Joe."

"Your dad was a fine man, Hunter. Oh, how he

bragged about you." The teenaged boy, his shoulders set as square as a cabinet, shaking more hands than he'd ever shaken before. "You made him proud, don't you ever doubt that."

"We'll be praying for ya'll."

"Brenda, I'm sorry."

"Let us know if there's anything we can do."

"If you need help cleaning out everything, will you call?"

"Joe will be missed."

"Oh, yes. Good job, Sam. Sam?"

Somewhere during this, Sam had stopped listening. The words all ran together after awhile. He'd turned himself off and gone on to something else. He was lost inside the hum, that familiar blurring. The question of his heart would be something he would ask over and over again as he lay awake during the nights to come.

Why does love always end?

CHAPTER NINE

"Wouldn't you consider spending some time with him, Sam?" Brenda asked as they sat across from each other at her kitchen table, their knees almost touching, as the fresh light of morning shimmered on the curtains. "Maybe taking him somewhere?"

They were sharing chocolate éclairs and vegetable soup for breakfast—balanced diet of champions, provided by a mixture of the Covenant Heights Women's Fellowship and the local Ladies Guild. Sam had been rattling around in his own kitchen, feeding Ginny, when he'd started to wonder if Brenda had gotten into their safety-deposit box yet. The safety-deposit box led him to wonder if she had notified the bank that carried their mortgage yet, which led him to wonder if she'd thought to turn over Joe's records to their tax accountant. So here he'd come, checking on her.

She gestured with her spoon. "After everything that's happened, a change of scenery would do Hunter good."

"It would do you good, too. Why don't you two do something together?" Sam leveled his eyes at his sister pointedly, lifted his coffee mug and tilted it toward his mouth.

Brenda bit into an éclair, closed her eyes, chewed slowly. Watching the gingerly way she ate her pastry made Sam want to destroy his in three brutal bites.

When she swallowed finally, she said, "I'm worried about how this is affecting him. He holds everything in and then he explodes."

"Right." Another slurp of coffee. "We've seen that."

"Right."

Sam had not gone to the police yard to view his ruined Mustang. He'd decided that would be for the best. Sam cared for his nephew, would stand and support him as he faced his list of consequences. Sam also knew himself well enough to know this: his resentment was there, lying in ambush. He felt it rumbling, heard it whispering, and he tried not to listen. He did not want to close his eyes and see crumpled red steel.

Lord, I don't want to feel this way, but I do. There isn't anything I can do to make it go away, so you're going to have to take it.

As Sam sat across from his sister, the silence stretched to an uncomfortable length between them. He realized he was jiggling his knee. He picked the mug up, tilted it, and found nothing there.

"Where is Hunter, anyway?"

"Upstairs asleep. He'd sleep until three if I let him."

"But you don't let him, do you?"

"Sometimes." Brenda kept babbling away. "There isn't any way for me to leave. We're behind on what stores have preordered." She worked for a cottage industry that made scrapbook paraphernalia—*Gilded Memories*, as it was called—offered tiny plastic suitcase stickers that said *Bon Voyage*, 3-D yellow duckies with umbrellas, white cartoon blurbs so a person could write what someone in a photo might be thinking. "I missed so much work with Joe sick. They were wonderful. But I can't ask for any more time now. I need to help them a lot this summer. Make it up to them."

"You could go when the orders are finished, couldn't you?"

"Hunter couldn't go then, though. School starts."

"Oh." He leaned back in the kitchen chair and when Brenda furrowed her brows and frowned, he thought she was going to chide him. *Once a mother, always a mother,* he wanted to say. Their mother had lectured them about it, too.

"I'm not just talking this time, don't you realize? I'm

serious." Then, "You're the one who knows so much about people, Sam."

He straightened right up in the chair.

"You're the minister, the one with all the answers. You're the one with all the training to know what to say."

The only thing Sam wanted to say to Hunter this minute was that he was furious at him for stealing the Mustang and for driving like a maniac. Brenda's plea tumbled into him like a stone.

Lord, she's right. You called me to pastor. I'm supposed to be better *than this.*

"He's too hurt to listen to anybody else, but *God* would speak through you to him. He would listen, I know he would."

"Brenda."

"Have you even *talked* to Hunter since the other night?"

"No." He set his mug down hard. "Did you expect me to? After what happened, I thought *Hunter* would be the one to speak to *me.* I thought an apology might be forthcoming."

"I apologized," she said inanely.

"No," he said. "I expected an apology from *him.* He *owes* me that much."

The anger in her face was unfair, yet it didn't surprise him. He knew her emotions were raw and any small thing could set her off. But it was *his* life, too, not some appointment he could walk away from toward the end of the day. Brenda's reaction was contagious. Or maybe, really, she had caught the anger from him. Because it was there, knotting inside him, taking his breath away.

"For heaven's sake, Sam. We've been through so much. Don't you think you could be less concerned about what he owes you?" She splayed both hands on the table, bit her lower lip, and leaned forward as if she were measuring him. She sighed, her shoulders rising, staying raised, until they fell like a beach toy being deflated.

The plate of éclairs sat like a blockade between them. On the counter to Sam's left, the Mr. Coffee made one last spit, its hot plate hissing. The clock hand above her head ticked off the seconds with sharp, stiff jerks.

"I'm not asking you to take Joe's place, you know. Nobody could do that."

"I wasn't thinking of it that way."

Sam had a sudden flicker of his life with Brenda, little sister tagging along behind him, pesky as always, giving her opinions of everything he did, organizing things, asking for things, slowing him down.

She had tricked him, yes, she had, plain and simple. All those years when he'd wanted Brenda to get out of his way, and here she was, still needing things from him. Here she was, still calling on him at every turn.

"You know how things can happen with boys this age. They do everything to impress their friends. They hide what they're feeling behind drinking and being aggressive and going wild."

"Yes."

"You know how easy it is for them to do something wrong and that one wrong choice can affect them forever."

Sam got up to pour more coffee. He held the carafe toward her. When she didn't respond he drained it into his own mug.

"Maybe he's feeling that God took his father away because God's *angry* with him about something."

Sam set the mug soundly on the table, stared at it, turned the handle until it pointed toward him.

"You know how thin that line is," Brenda went on. "Kids fall off the ledge on either side and can't recover from it. It depends on what they feel about themselves, what they think they're capabilities are. That's what I'm afraid of."

Sam agreed with all she was telling him. Brenda's reasoning pinned him to the wall the way a dart zinged in on a bull's-eye. There was only one thing she was wrong about, only one thing that she did not see: *he's too hurt to listen to anybody else, but God would speak through you.*

God doesn't seem to be using me much lately. Did you notice that?

"I'm afraid he'll keep making the wrong choices. You know what happens, Sam. Once a teenager starts going downhill, he goes straight down if there's nothing to stop him."

Sam felt suddenly light-headed, not knowing if it was from early-morning éclairs or from being tired or from the weight of her request. "Brenda, you asked me to do

Joe's service when I would have rather been beside you in the pew, and I *did* the service. You wanted me to take your cat to the vet when it was time to put him to sleep, and I did that. You asked me to be in the room with Joe when Hunter was born and I did that." Sam was just getting warmed up. "You call every time you need help moving Mom's piano, and I do *that.* You wanted me to talk to Joe about buying a house and I did that. You asked me if I'd be the one to find the right place for Mom and I did *that.*"

"I know."

"You're so busy thinking of things I can do for you that you don't realize I've lost a best friend, too."

"I know I asked you all those things." He hated the way she sounded betrayed. Her words were smooth and dry. "I didn't know you'd been keeping score."

"I wasn't."

Spending time with Hunter might not have been too much for him any other time. But being responsible for his nephew right now felt like the last straw, something that would break him. It felt like too much while Sam struggled with this doubt in himself, his misgivings about in his own capacity to access God's power.

"He's hurting about Joe, maybe worse than we are. When Hunter hit that cow and killed it, I don't think you know this, but it was the first time he was able to cry."

Sam rose, deliberately swished water in his mug. "I'm sorry." He set the mug on the sideboard. "I have to go."

All through the years, he'd recognized the importance of not failing his sister. And now, look what he had to do.

"Sam? What are you telling me?"

Their disappointments hung in the air like dust, swirling between them.

It's not that I don't trust God anymore. It's that I don't trust me.

"You need to be the one who's there for your son, Brenda. I don't have anything to give him."

CHAPTER TEN

As Sam filed into the Covenant Heights boardroom Tuesday night for the monthly church business meeting, he carried a burden of guilt with him. All day, he'd weighed the cost of deserting his sister. All day, he'd berated himself for feeling empty and dry and unable to minister to his nephew, the one person who, among the others, probably needed him the most.

Sam wanted nothing more than to have this meeting go smoothly so he could return to the house, sequester himself inside his leather chair with Ginny nestled beside his feet, and nurse his guilt even further.

All began well. The deacon board worked their way through the approval of Mary Grace's minutes and the treasurer's report and the adoption of the next year's Sunday school curricula. They discussed the building-and-ground committee's intention to accept bids for the parking-lot lights, extolled the virtues of the Concerto

II Orchestral organ, and authorized the youth pastor to research a youth mission trip to Matamoros, Mexico, for next July. They decided, due to impressive attendance, to continue the early-morning contemporary praise-and-worship service, complete with Ian Barker's snare drums. They set the final date for the Christmas cantata. Then, they even called an executive session and, upon its conclusion, voted to award Mary Grace a modest and well-deserved salary increase.

Not until the bedraggled group began shoving away from the table and piling papers into notebooks did Grant Ransom say in a measured voice, "Sam, we haven't adjourned. There is another item we have to deal with."

"Well, someone go ahead and adjourn us," Dave Hawthorne said, glancing at his watch. "I wanted to catch the last of the Cardinals game."

But no one did. Chairs scraped toward the table again. Mary Grace leaned forward beside Sam, her red hair shining in the overhead lights. She flipped open her tablet again and, with a heavy sigh, readied her pen to take more notes. "You know what this is about, Pastor Tibbits?" she whispered. "Grant didn't say anything to me."

Sam shook his head. "Me, neither." He shrugged. And in that short moment, he remained blessedly unaware of the events about to ensue.

Mary Grace smelled like oranges. Grapefruit, maybe. Something citrus that seemed to match her hair. She, above all the others, understood his aspirations for

Covenant Heights and for its congregation. In that short moment, Sam admitted that he found her presence both pleasant and reassuring beside him.

Grant, sitting three chairs down, pulled a yellow legal pad from beneath his arm. He tamped the pad on the table and, as seconds ticked by and Grant hesitated to speak, Sam began to wonder if something might be awry.

He glanced at Mary Grace again and, this time, it was her turn to shrug.

Sam was sure no one in the Covenant Heights congregation loved this little church more than the Ransom family. When Grant's father-in-law had died, Grant had set up a good amount of their inheritance as an endowment fund to keep vacation Bible school functioning in perpetuity. Every Wednesday at lunchtime, Grant left his own office and came to the church. In forty-five minutes' time, no matter how bad the weather, he would insist that Sam settle on a sermon topic, would sort through the big plastic letters in the storage room, and would post Sunday's upcoming title—things like WHEN A WISE MAN COMES TO CALL or THE THREE STEPS TO FINDING YOUR DESTINY—on the billboard beside the street.

Most important of all, Grant had always been the one to stop by Sam's study and say, "Buddy, what you say we head over to Saylorville Lake and throw some rocks in? Let your dog get her feet wet? I know you could use a break and I could, too."

Grant tamped his notes against the table again and

started to speak. For a moment, Sam was distracted by the open window behind him. The summer night drifted in, soft and sweet smelling, and Sam began thinking of rolling down the windows in his car on the way home, listening to music. Grant's words floated along toward him the same way he imagined the songs.

". . . everyone knows . . . care for this church . . . deep love for its pastor . . ."

Sam made himself focus. *Okay. Okay. What is this, friend?*

". . . jeopardize the . . ." Grant was saying, "I would never jeopardize the future of anything here."

Oh, then, of course, Sam knew. The deacon board wanted to make certain he knew where they stood on his "meal for the homeless" issue. Grant's next words confirmed Sam's guess. "We all see how you're pushing this, Sam. You need to know that several members of your deacon board do not think this is the direction that the church ought to go."

"The Father is calling us to befriend the friendless, Grant. I don't know how anyone can disagree with that."

"None of us opposes the idea in principle, you know that. But, as a church, we can't be all things to all people. We have others already worshiping with us who have needs."

"I see." *And I see more,* Sam thought.

Maybe he was wrong this time. Maybe something inside his own life, a compulsion he didn't recognize, was causing him to feel this avid draw toward those living in the Des Moines streets. Maybe when Sam had been small, too young to remember, a street person had shown some kindness to him. But he didn't want to turn away from this, an impulse within him that mirrored other impulses that had felt supernatural, something that might prod his flock toward the explicitly divine.

When Sam had invited the homeless man named Kil, who he'd met at a bus kiosk, to services this past Sunday, he had done so in hopes that others might meet Kil and be drawn into their pastor's vision. That idea, however, hadn't gone over well. Yes, the man had found a seat in the third-row pew this past Sunday—in the Hawthornes' regular spot. Lester Kraft (wonderful, wonderful Lester) had hugged Kil in welcome during the greeting time. But Kil hadn't smelled good. He had sniffed stridently and made loud comments while Sam delivered the message. He had rocked back and forth in the pew. During the singing of hymns, he had shed what remained of his shoes, had shoved them beneath the pew in front of him, and had wiggled his dirty toes.

"I'll admit," Sam blurted out. "I invited him. If you heard his story—"

Sam had asked Kil questions about his life while they'd stood together, waiting for the city bus. Kil had come from Chicago, where he'd kept his earthly belongings in a shopping cart. One night a teenager had torched his shopping cart and by the time Kil's street family had extinguished the flames, everything he owned had been gone. His only friend, for a number of months, had been a beagle named Bench. Kil had unchained the dog from the back of a truck only to find out, after Bench happily and opportunely followed him along the streets for two weeks, the dog's name engraved on its collar was short for "Approach the Bench." Kil had untied a drug search dog worth thousands.

"—if you heard his story, you might feel differently about it."

"I've heard plenty of stories about the homeless in Des Moines. I've given money to the shelters myself."

The Scriptures, the images, the arguments had all been engraved deeply within Sam. *What is it about this, Grant?* he might have asked. *Are you just afraid of having the homeless finding a refuge here? Or does it go deeper? Would you not welcome someone from the poorer side of Des Moines? Or someone who wasn't born and raised in Iowa?*

Sam might have quoted something from the Bible. Psalm 113 came to mind. *He raises the poor from the dust and lifts the needy from the ash heap.* Or he might have asked, *Since when have you been willing to leave things the way they are, Grant? Since when have you been satisfied with the status quo?*

But Sam held his breath, aching inside, and let all these comments go unspoken between them.

"You know my family supports Covenant Heights financially. But we might have to rethink things. We may not want to commit this much to a church that cares more for entertaining vagrants than it does for its own congregation."

This intense calling to encourage his flock, this need to reach out to people like Kil, had begun well before Sam and Brenda had helped their dad move their mom into the retirement center. It had been with him well before Joe had fallen ill. He had been pushing for this during Joe's emotional and taxing funeral, Sam's helping Brenda, and Hunter wrecking the Mustang. His desire to reach out to the homeless had remained a firm certitude the entire time Sam had prayed for Joe's healing. Now, it was the only thing Sam had left.

"There are agencies in place to take care of the homeless, Sam. These people are not fundamentally the church's problem."

"I believe this goes deeper than being an agency, Grant. I believe we'd be reaching out in love to the most unreachable, unsaved in Des Moines." Then, "You would withdraw your financial support over this? The Ransom endowment?" Sam knew this was the wrong way to put the question, but Sam suddenly felt too exhausted to measure his words. "After everything our friendship has meant to both of us?"

"Don't take this to a personal level, Sam. This is about the *church*."

For one split second, one curious moment that Sam couldn't decipher, his deacon and friend examined a thumbnail. "Your energy level, Sam. We see that you're tired. Ever since Joe died, you aren't as effective with the congregation as you could be."

"I see."

"The other day when I walked into your office, you

were sitting with your head on your desk."

"Yes."

"You aren't paying attention to details. The lighting of the parking area, for instance. And now you're talking about bringing in another ministry, something that will drain you further." From some distant, hollow place, Sam heard Grant proceeding. "There are those of us here, Sam," he said very gently, very carefully, "who think you need to take a sabbatical from Covenant Heights."

Sam lifted his chin and stared at Grant. For the first time he noticed the quiet around the table. "What do you *mean?*"

"We mean that you need a break from the church. You know. Something of a vacation."

And something else whispered back to him, *It means they're not satisfied with you anymore.*

No one moved. Dave Hawthorne, who must not have known about this beforehand, stared in shock at his St. Louis Cardinals cap beside his arm. Sam heard Mary Grace's breath come in a painful rush. Harvey Mitler, another deacon, stared at the lid of his Bic ballpoint as if it might shoot off and fly across the room any second.

"Have I done something wrong? Have I offended anyone? Grant, have I offended *you?*"

Silence.

"Am I repeating too many of the same jokes from the pulpit or what?"

The warm breeze from the open window made everything feel damp, the computer beneath his fingers, the skin on the base of his neck. "At this point," Grant said, "we think we are better off as a congregation without you."

"We?" Sam asked. "Who is *we?*"

"Your deacon board. We had a quorum. We voted."

What gave Sam the oddest feeling—the most painful thing of all, really—was realizing that this had been discussed among his colleagues, whispered in hallways, brought up over lunches, dissected over cell phones, and he had never had any idea.

"I see," Sam said, parroting himself, hating his voice for sounding like an automaton. His throat had squeezed shut and he couldn't seem to force it open. "How long?" he finally managed. "How long do you want me to stay away?"

"We were thinking, oh, two, three months. Enough for you to figure out what the priorities of Covenant Heights need to be."

"You're expecting me to change my mind?"

"We're hoping you'll decide to focus in some other area."

But who is going to preach Sunday if I'm not here? Who is going to talk to Lester about the carbon dating of the earth and Dottie about the faith it has taken to trust God with her son and the lonely man in the park who is grieving his dog Bench?

Sam wondered if there would even be a job *left* for him when he returned, if they wanted him to be gone for so long.

Why take a sabbatical? Where would I even go?

"Who would take my place? An associate? Would someone step up?"

"The board has already contacted several people. We've found someone who'll serve as interim pastor. We're bringing someone in. Someone who—"

"—will use my study. Do my job."

What are they going to do without me for three months?

Who is going to eat all those casseroles if I don't?

Fear began to needle at him. Suddenly, Sam wondered if he would have a position here when he returned. No matter how Sam worked to remind himself that fear wasn't from the Lord, that his Father must have a reason for this, the questions flew at him.

If anything happened so that I wasn't a pastor, how could I be anything else?

"You understand that it's a space issue. If we had space to put him in a different office, we would do that."

Long after the others had left for home that night, long after Grant had driven away and Dave had gone to try and catch the bottom of the ninth in the Cardinal's game, Sam remained at the conference table, staring at his hands, shocked.

Shocked that Grant had threatened to withdraw financial support, which felt almost treacherous.

Shocked that tomorrow morning when he got out of bed and began to plan, nothing would be the same as it had been today.

Uncertainty began its first niggling assault upon him. Perhaps the deacons were right and he was wrong, perhaps he had somehow misinterpreted his calling, lost his focus. Perhaps they saw clearly and Sam's own vision, which he depended on for his very survival in this pastorate, had grown murky.

This is everything I know how to be, Lord.

I wouldn't know how to do any of this differently.

A vast library of reference books and tattered choir music and twenty years' worth of teaching materials lined the high dark shelves around him. The room had never felt so empty, so heavy and meaningless, so devoid of sound.

Yet he was not quite alone. Mary Grace had been the only person who did not scurry away from him the moment the meeting adjourned. After the others had filed out, she had remained in her chair.

Sam had readied himself for her outburst of immediate sympathy. But that had not come. The woman who lit up the church hallways like a bright jungle creature and who teased him about his fake office plants now ministered to him with her simple, silent presence. She offered him neither encouragement nor solace.

Even in his pain, how grateful he was that Mary Grace understood. Sam's struggle with this unforeseen doubt took him beyond words.

CHAPTER ELEVEN

Sam and his dad walked together Tuesday morning, something father and son had made a pact to do once a week. They tramped side by side in two ruts of farm road that cut across Hamby's cornfields, the seven o'clock August sun illuminating the green stalks with a golden glow. For a long time they didn't talk. Their steps were long and powerful, their arms swinging in cadence, matching each other stride for stride. Their feet swished through the grass and, when they made it back to the Tibbits old house, their sneakers would be wet with dew.

Ginny ran ahead of them, bounding in zigzags among the stalks, sending cobwebs and corn silk scattering through the air like ribbons.

As Sam marched beside Edward Tibbits, doubts assaulted him like physical blows. How long had he faithfully battled for what he thought was right for the church?

Yes, he finally admitted, *I'm grieving. Fatigued. Burned out.*

If not for these things, his doubt might not have defeated him. He just didn't think he could fight anymore.

If Grant is right and I'm wrong, if I'm not hearing from the Lord now, have I ever really heard from the Lord at all?

When they arrived at the house, Ginny slurped up

water from a bowl Edward kept there for her. Their breath was still coming in heavy, labored gasps. They stepped inside the kitchen that hadn't changed since Sam was a boy. The air inside felt stuffy, so Edward opened the window over the sink and went to switch on the attic fan.

His dad returned and Sam was acutely aware that he was still standing in the same spot Edward had left him. He never could walk into this kitchen without missing his mother. He swallowed hard. "How is she doing, Dad?"

"Not too well, son, I'm afraid." Sam's father tugged a tea towel off the rack, mopped his sweaty face, and hung it right back up again. "She didn't have a thing to say when I showed her those." He pointed to the photos he'd left on the counter.

"What are they?"

"Old vacation pictures. From Piddock Beach."

"Can I see them?"

"Sure."

Edward slid the entire stack toward Sam and they fanned out of their own accord. Sam picked them up and began to thumb through them.

"Those trips were always so much fun. I thought if I took them to the nursing home and talked about them, your mom would remember."

"And she didn't?"

Edward shook his head and reached for the orange juice carton. "No."

"Dad. I'm sorry."

As he watched his dad pour orange juice into a glass, Sam could see his hand shaking. Sam stood, studying that trembling hand, a hand that had once been sure and strong. Sam caught himself wanting to step to the sink and touch his father's arm and make it stop. But that seemed wrong, too, even to acknowledge it. He turned to the pictures again and pretended he had not seen.

"Dad. Look at this. Do you remember this swim cap of Mom's? Brenda and I used to beg her to wear it because those rubber flowers came off and we got to dive for them in the drain."

"Which swim cap? Oh, *that*."

They chuckled their way through pictures of Edward's baggy Bermuda shorts and a short-sleeved Hawaiian shirt that looked like a billboard for pineapples. They laughed at Sam's buzzed hair. At Terrie's waist that looked about as big around as a candlestick in her skirt and broad leather belt. At Brenda's cat's-eye sunglasses with bright yellow stones arrowing from each of her temples while she stood under the shade of a myrtlewood tree.

There came a photograph of Terrie rolling Brenda's hair and they made rude comments about the brush curlers Terrie had been using. They remembered Brenda's screaming while her mother impaled her head with each pink holding pin. "Why on earth were they doing their hair in the first place, Dad? We were at the *beach*."

"Oh, you know." Edward replaced the orange juice in the refrigerator. *"Women."*

114

Edward's statement, *Women,* brought them full circle to where this conversation had begun. Their laughter died. Father and son eyed each other somberly. "Such a shame, isn't it," Edward asked, "that Terrie can't be there for Brenda right now? She could sure use her mother at a time like this. The way she's lost Joe, and all."

"I know."

"Brenda could sure use her mother's advice, trying to raise that son of hers."

"I know."

Sam laid the photographs on the counter again and Edward picked them up. "This is the one I was sure would get the reaction from her," he said, pulling out one particular snapshot. Sam glanced over to see one Brownie Starmite photo of Terrie on the bridge of the *Westerly,* an awful grimace on her face, holding up the dead weight of a lingcod. "This was the only time I convinced her to go in the boat with us and catch something. She was always running into town to go shopping instead of fishing, remember?"

Sam nodded.

"You ever wonder what happened to those McCarts?" Edward asked. "We used to have so much fun on those boats."

"No," Sam lied.

"What a life, hanging out at the wharf for a living, bringing in fish for the tourists. Why, if I had to do it all over again, I'd . . ."

Sam waited, thinking his father meant to finish the sentence. When he didn't, Sam broke the silence.

"What? What would you do all over again?"

"Oh, I don't know, Son. I was just talking."

"You ever wish you could go back, Dad? Knowing how things turned out? Do you ever wonder if you had the chance to live those years again with Mom, if you'd do it differently?"

Edward shifted his weight from one foot to the other, propped himself against the green-tile counter with his hip. Sam could see sweat soaking through the chest of his father's fray-necked T-shirt, a wet shape where the shirt read 5K TOWN RACE: A RUN TO WIPE OUT CRIME.

"Why ask a question like that?"

"If there might have been one moment that changed something, would you go back and change it now?"

Edward sounded almost angry. "Drive myself crazy like that? Trying to figure out which moment it might have been that altered everything? Are you kidding?"

Sam slumped in the kitchen chair where he'd sat ten thousand times before and pried the heel of one sneaker off with the toe of the other. No sense bothering with shoelaces. He peeled off his socks, the odor of which made him wince, and a smattering of tiny rocks skittered across the wooden floor.

"Is that the way you've decided things are, Sam? One person doing one right thing at the right time?"

Sam tried to clean up the tiny pebbles that had fallen out of his shoes. He raked them into a pile with his hands and looked in the broom closet for the dustpan.

"You think everything depends on that?" his father asked.

Sam swept the dirt into the pan, dumped it into the trash. Then, he turned each filthy sneaker upside-down and pounded it against the trashcan rim.

"I would have thought, with the things you profess to believe in, Sam, that you wouldn't place so much stock in your own power."

Edward dealt the photograph onto the table the same way he would deal an ace. Sam glanced down and there, in front of him, was a picture of Aubrey McCart.

"You want to tell me what's going on in your life, son? Why you walked the whole trail this morning without telling me one story about those people over at the church that you care so much about?"

Sam returned the dustpan to the closet without speaking.

"You didn't say much at all while we were walking."

When Sam had emptied his sneakers into the trash, he'd noticed the can was full. Now he lifted the bag from the can, cinched it, and knotted it tight.

"I'd say that means something's up."

Sam made it almost to the back door with it clutched in his arms before he stopped and stared at the ceiling. "What would you think if I traveled somewhere, Dad? Would you and Brenda be able to handle things with Mom if I left town for a few weeks?"

Their eyes met at last. Edward waited, and Sam knew his dad understood there was something more.

"They've asked me to take a sabbatical. I don't have any other choice but to go."

"Son."

"I feel like I'm running away." The hinges rasped as Sam shoved open the screen and carted the bag outside. When he returned, his dad held the door open for him. "I feel like I should be there right now, fighting for my position, telling Grant Ransom he's made an awful mistake."

"Maybe the Father isn't calling you to fight."

"Maybe that's the only thing I know how to do." Then, "I've always believed that fighting defines the very essence of faith."

"Maybe it isn't your fighting he wants anymore, son. Maybe it's your relinquishing the fight to him."

Outside, an empty dump truck rattled past on the road. Ginny had her big head lodged beneath a chair, trying to reach one of her huge collection of balls. Sam dug it out for her and lobbed it across the room. Ginny bounded after it and caught it mid-bounce. Edward crossed the kitchen, clapped a hand across his son's shoulders in consolation.

"I'll come to terms with it on my own, Dad. Now it's you and Mom I'm worried about."

"Since when do you get to worry about us? We're the ones who are supposed to worry about you."

"Since—" But Sam didn't finish the sentence. Because they both already knew what he would say. *Since Mom stopped remembering.*

"You've been taking care of everyone else but yourself for a long time, boy. We'll be fine. I don't want you to worry about us."

"If she had a good day, if she wanted to see me, I wouldn't be nearby."

"If she asks, I'll tell her where you are. I'll tell her what you're doing. I'll tell her you've been a good fighter for a long time."

The old photograph from Piddock Beach still lay on the table. At last, Sam picked it up and looked at it.

Edward said, "That girl. What do you suppose ever happened to her?"

Sam stared at it without saying a word.

"What was her name? I don't remember. You two were such good friends back then. Andrea? Alice? Alice McCart?"

"No, Dad. Aubrey. It was Aubrey."

"Cute little thing, always hanging around those boats and wanting to help her father."

"She was a good friend."

"You two lost touch, didn't you? She left town or something. I remember now."

After all these years, how odd it seemed to speak Aubrey's name. It shocked Sam that even listening to his father mentioning her in this small, trivial way brought him pleasure. He was instantly catapulted back to summers along the coast, the chime-like clamor of fishing-boat riggings on windy days, the rustle of the dunegrass, the flow of the ocean against the shore.

"You decided where you're going on this sabbatical?" his dad asked.

"Guess I could go anywhere I wanted."

"I guess you could, at that."

Edward began working his way out of his T-shirt. "I'd better get going. Let you get to the office."

"I'd better head in that direction."

Sam returned to the chair and began to loosen his laces. He slid one foot in, then another, yanked the strings taut. For a long moment, he focused on them as wholly as he'd focus on rethreading a guitar string. "I'll stop by and see Mom before I leave."

"That would be good."

Sam had, as yet, to tie the laces into bows. His fingers remained still a long time. "I don't doubt God, Dad. I doubt myself," he said. "I don't know if I've done anything right to this point."

Edward removed his keys from the peg beside the door. Sam finished his shoes, grabbed his jacket, whistled for Ginny.

"You remember when we were trying to make the best decisions for your mom, Sam? You remember when you said to me, 'If you make a decision in honest belief, Dad, even if it's the wrong decision, God can get things on track again?'"

"I don't remember saying that to you."

"Well, you did."

On their way out, Sam stopped to examine the snapshot one last time, and decided it must have been taken when Aubrey was thirteen. She'd had a certain look about her at thirteen. He would never forget the mystery of it, as if she were ages wiser than she'd been at twelve; as if she'd crossed some threshold, as if, already, she'd journeyed to a place from which she could not return. She wasn't fourteen yet in this picture; Sam was certain. Other changes had come to her when she was fourteen—*woman* changes, which had made him the slightest bit uncomfortable, changes he would never forget.

How many years ago had that been? Sam started to add, then grinned with irony when he realized the years went beyond addition. He would be forced to multiply instead.

"Makes sense, a man's biggest doubt being himself," his dad said. "I've been feeling the same thing about your mom. How scary it is to go forward, knowing you're incapable of something, knowing you've got to do it anyway."

Sam bit his lower lip, nodded his head slowly. "Nothing's turned out the way I thought it would."

"Doubt can feel a lot like fear. I don't want you to be afraid of yourself, Sam. God wouldn't want it, either."

"Advice," Sam said, finally laughing. "I knew you'd end up giving me advice."

He waved his dad good-bye in the driveway and pulled the car door shut behind him. And as Sam drove home to begin packing, he kept seeing the thirteen-year-old girl in the picture, her brown hair riffling against her shoulders, the jetty in the background. If she spoke at all, he knew this is what she would be saying, "Did you know that a cat has thirty-two muscles in each ear?" Or, "Did you know that human beings are born without kneecaps?"

It felt uncanny how imagining her voice drew him back, how Audrey's green eyes still seemed to peer into his soul.

Mary Grace Pokorny was the last person Sam spoke to before he left town. He was on his way out the door. He wouldn't have answered except her number came up on his cell.

"Hello?" Then, "Mary Grace?" after he'd waited what seemed an inordinate amount of time. "What's wrong? Have I forgotten something?"

It had taken him precious little time to set things to rights in his office. He'd thrown away the half-empty bottle of V-8 Splash he kept stashed beneath his desk chair. He'd draped his vestment over a wire hanger and left it on the coat rack so the interim pastor could find it. He'd stowed his guitar in its case, fastened the clasps with three quick snaps, and had lugged it out to the car. That had been the extent of his packing.

"You haven't forgotten a thing." Then, "I just—"

"What?"

"I just need to talk to you before you head out."

It occurred to Sam that there were certainly things he needed to say to Mary Grace, too. He needed to thank her for being his confidante, someone he'd been able to trust with the matters of his flock. He needed to thank her for her laughter, which often strengthened him. He needed to thank her for looking beyond the superficial and advising him when something subtle begged to be seen. He'd been so focused on his own hurt that he hadn't stopped to think how this would affect her.

"Thank you for everything, Mary Grace. You've been such a great help around this place."

"You talk like you aren't coming back."

The low, measured tone of her voice left him puzzled. Sam hadn't been certain how she'd respond to his leave-taking, whether she'd argue against it or express pity toward him or tell him that she thought he was right to go.

She did none of these things. Instead she said in that subdued voice, "I want you to take care of yourself. Do you hear me?"

He wasn't certain what he should say. "Are you lecturing me about this?" he asked.

"Yes."

"You almost didn't catch me. I was just on my way."

"Keep your cell with you," she said. "Just in case something comes up. You could call—"

"I will." He realized he was pressing his cell tight against his skull.

"Sam?"

He fumbled with his phone, readjusting it against his ear. "Yes?"

"You remember you're not leaving behind just a place or a problem, Sam. You remember you're leaving behind people who care about you."

CHAPTER TWELVE

Hunter slumped on the passenger side of the car with his arms crossed behind the headrest and his sneakers buttressed against the dashboard. His cap brim, which he wore tilted toward his ear, bore a graffiti logo for some rap singer that, for all Sam could tell, might as well have been in Japanese. Hunter, Mr. Sullen and Silent, had kept his eyes narrow and aimed straight ahead ever since he'd pitched his duffel into the trunk and they'd driven away.

Not even Ginny, who nosed around in the seat behind them and occasionally planted her head on Hunter's shoulder, had been able to make him thaw.

They'd headed westward into the sun and the heat of the day, with the air-conditioning bellowing to keep up. Now that the light had dissipated behind the broad Nebraska grasslands, Sam no longer had to squint into the glare. He slowed a little before they reached I-80 and cracked the windows so Ginny could poke her head out and lap up some fresh air. A whiff of feed lot wafted in. "Ah, the open road," Sam said. "Ginny, now there's a—"

But he stopped. He'd been about to say, *Ginny, now there's a fragrance for you to roll in, my dear.* But he realized any mention of cattle would bring them onto perilous ground. *Hey, Hunter. That smell remind you of Omaha Steaks? You suppose that's what became of the poor cow you bashed into with my Mustang?*

Sam snapped his lips shut and drove on for another fifteen miles without saying anything at all.

For the umpteenth time since they'd left Iowa, Sam found himself thinking of Covenant Heights. No matter how hard he tried, he could not stop thinking about his church. It was Tuesday. What would they be doing on Tuesday? Well, the staff meeting, for one thing.

Stop it, Sam. No reason to torture yourself. He sent up a prayer for them and called it good.

He unwrapped his fingers from the steering wheel and closed them over it again. He made himself focus on Hunter instead.

"We could listen to your music. I wouldn't mind."

But Hunter didn't answer, not a grunt or anything. It was Sam's fifth attempt in as many hours to start a conversation with the boy. Hunter stared straight ahead, chewing his bottom lip, slapping out some sporadic angry rhythm on his knee.

So Sam turned on his music instead. He slipped a CD into the player and turned the volume loud. "Mocking-bird," the duet between James Taylor and Carole King. Sam burst into song. "Mock-*yeah!* ing-*yeah!* bird-*yeah!* Yeah-*yeah!*"

"Okay," Hunter gasped in desperation. "We'll listen to *my* music."

"I thought so," Sam said. "Give me something and I'll put it in."

Hunter seemed to use every ounce of energy he could muster to heave himself off of his rear end, push Ginny out of the way, and dig around for his CD case. He

125

swung back to the front seat with a black nylon holder that was three times as thick as Sam's Bible. He flipped through the plastic sleeves until he found something acceptable.

"A seatbelt would be good, too," Sam said, before he realized that would bring them to dangerous territory again. *Good thing you were wearing your seatbelt the night you wrecked my Mustang.*

Hunter picked something with red letters, slid it into the player and instantly the car filled with sound—the same furious beat and timbre as the tensions raging between them. The CD played through three different so-called "tunes" before Hunter slouched against the headrest and heaved a sigh loud enough to be heard across three counties. "I don't see the point of this. I really don't."

Sam kept his aviator sunglasses trained on the interstate, his spine rigid, his mouth in a careful, emotionless set.

"This is stupid." Then, with his head thrown against the headrest again, "There isn't even anything *out* here."

Sam settled his shoulders lower against the seat, held the steering wheel at arm's length. "Oh, we'll get where we're headed eventually. You'll see."

Hunter punched up the volume another notch, folded his arms across his chest, and stared out at the passing sea of crops and meadow.

Scotland, Sam told himself. If he'd had the money to really travel, he could have gone to Scotland. He'd always thought if anything happened like this and he ended up on the open road with no one to answer to except himself and the heavenly Father, he would go somewhere he'd never been. He pictured himself searching out his heritage, listening to people with new ideas, considering things he hadn't thought of before. He'd try to see himself out of context, maybe buy everyone wool sweaters.

"Look," Sam said, trying again, "I was hoping we could make something of this time together."

Hunter jostled his weight from one hip to the other. "No, you weren't."

"Hunter—"

"You're lying."

That accusation made for another ten miles of silence between them. Sam waited a good while, worrying, before he pursued this conversation further. "I don't know what makes you say a thing like that."

"I heard you when you told Mom you didn't want to take me anywhere. Don't you know?"

Sam checked his blind spot, signaled, pulled around a combine that was bouncing along the shoulder of the road.

"I was awake," the boy said. "I was listening. So, let's not fake each other out, okay?"

Things changed for me, Sam wanted to tell the boy. But he was sick of making excuses. "Okay," Sam said instead.

"I heard my mother ask if you'd spend time with me. I heard you tell her you didn't want to."

Hunter's CD had ended and started over again. He ejected it and slipped it inside the plastic sleeve. "You going to make us drive all night?"

"We'll stop in a while and find a motel."

"If we have to go to a beach, we ought to go to a *real* beach. Someplace with a water park and people my age and other things to do."

"What part of the Oregon coastline, Hunter, do you think is not real?" But it hit Sam then. He barely missed a beat before he said, "You're talking girls in bikinis, aren't you, sir? More like—"

"Cancun."

"Ah. I see. Cancun."

"Or Florida."

"Yes."

"Swimming in Oregon, you freeze to death. You get hypothermia. You'd probably die. You'd have to wear a wet suit or just be plain dumb."

"Well." Sam decided it was dusky enough to remove his glasses. He dropped them on the console beside Hunter's leg and rubbed the bridge of his nose. "Call me just plain dumb."

"*You* went swimming in Oregon?"

"All the time. It took bravery, of course. But I was very brave."

Or stupid, Sam guessed his nephew wanted to say. *Really, really stupid.* But Hunter shuffled his huge Nikes under the cooling vent and only said, "Whatever."

They stopped to fill up at a gas station that doubled as a campground. As Hunter worked the pump, Sam snapped Ginny's leash on and took her walking along a grassy knoll. At least three dozen motor homes and tents stood lined next to each other below him. A number of fire pits on the lawn were alight with moving, golden sprays of flame. Aluminum camp chairs stood at right angles to each other on the manicured grass. Everywhere Sam turned there were gatherings of people, laughter and conversation, the muted smell of grilling food.

Who could say what it was that started the ache inside him? Ginny must have sensed something; dogs do that. She pressed herself up hard against his knee.

But the boundary that had kept Sam's isolation at bay had disappeared. His sense of hiding in darkness, of watching others assembled around warmth, overcame him. *Father. Yahweh? One who loves me? Are you there?* Suddenly he'd never felt so wounded and raw.

Inside the glare of the store, the cash register was lined with mechanical hamsters dressed in karate garb. Sam had seen them; you pressed a paw and the hamster twirled its num-chuck and sang "Kung-Fu Fighting" for way too long. He could turn them on all at once, maybe get a smile out of Hunter. Common sense won out, though. That would embarrass the kid so much he'd want to sink through the floor.

"You hungry? Want something to eat?" He could see the top of Hunter's head browsing the snack aisle.

Sam found himself a cellophane-wrapped sandwich with a slab of rubbery cheese and turkey that had gone gray. Hunter arrived with something equally as healthy—a bag of beef jerky, a burrito, and a Mountain Dew. Sam handed over his credit card. "Any place close to spend the night if you *don't* have a camper?" he asked the clerk as he signed the receipt and pocketed his wallet.

"Oh, there's plenty of motels up ahead. There's a Little America just after you get past Cheyenne. About forty more miles, I'd say. Can't miss it, place is lit up like a Christmas tree at night."

"Thanks."

Sam hesitated with door handle in hand when they arrived back at the car. He looked at Hunter, who was already ripping into the bag of jerky with his teeth. It would be the perfect time for Sam to suggest his nephew help him drive, the perfect time for him to pitch the keys over the hood and say, "Why don't you take the wheel for a while, kid?"

As a result of the accident, Hunter's license would be suspended for at least three months. Even if the boy *had* been able to share driving, handing over that duty would have implied too much trust. It would have implied a sense of camaraderie that the two did not share. Sam caught the keys inside his own fist and slid behind the wheel again. They drove away from the pump and left the canopy of harsh florescent light behind them. When they turned off the asphalt, the frontage road ran up a short hill to the green interstate sign. When they merged onto the highway, their head-lamps seemed alive and warm slipping into the night ahead of them.

CHAPTER THIRTEEN

If anyone were to stand on the outside of her life looking in, Aubrey McCart reasoned, that person would never suspect that her life might be less than satisfactory. Anyone looking in would see only a spotless, beautiful house, the living-room carpet as lush and cushioned as the golf-course turf that edged the patio. He would see the arrangement of *Town and Country* magazines on the coffee table and hear the sound of the children as they argued over who would have the next turn on the thick cedar swing set that Gary had built outside.

On Monday and Thursday of next week, the house-keeper would arrive. Giramina kept her own key. She would dust the furniture and polish the brass utensils beside the fireplace. She would rearrange the scads of stuffed animals and wash and iron the sheets. She would invade Billy's hamper—something so frightening that Aubrey had told her not to do it—and every soccer shirt and pair of jeans would be found neatly pressed and folded, sorted in his drawers.

It all seemed terribly normal, but today that deception would be forever destroyed.

Aubrey heard heavy, muffled thumping on the stairs. That would be Hannah, she knew, the youngest, bringing her suitcase down, the tatters of her pink blanket protruding from the zipper. Aubrey reached her arms out to assist, but the five-year-old veered wildly around her mother, saying, "I can do this *myself,*" as the wheels on her bag bumped across the seams in the hardwood floor. Billy bounded down next, headed straight for the door, his mouth set into a grim line. He clutched his soccer-ball pillow against his chest as if he were clutching a shield to protect himself from her.

Billy was the one she needed to intercept. "Where are your clothes?" she asked.

"In here." He hugged his pillow tighter.

"You're not taking enough, then. Not if it fits in there."

"I've got everything I need, Mom."

"Your toothbrush? Where's your toothbrush?"

"In here."

"Underwear?"

No answer.

She lowered her chin at him. "Billy?"

"I've got enough."

"How many?"

"Enough for two weeks."

"In your pillow."

"Yes."

"How many?" She kept him under arrest with her eyes.

"Two pairs," he conceded. "Mom, Aunt Emily's got a washer. I've *got* everything I *need.*"

Channing came trouncing down, ready for the airport, in a hip-hugger skirt shorter than the minis Aubrey used to wear, an off-the-shoulder sweater, and a pair of lambskin mukluks more appropriate for a ski resort than a flight to California. She wore her straight blond hair slung off to one side of her face. The braces on her teeth, flashing silver, were the only thing that pegged her at fifteen instead of twenty. Just watching her teenage daughter enter a room made Aubrey feel helpless.

Channing was the one Aubrey ached to touch. Hannah was still young enough to belong to her. If Aubrey timed it right with her young son, she could manage to capture him long enough for a little squeeze or slip him into her lap for one millisecond or capture that sweaty, irreplaceable scent of his hair. Channing liked to pretend she hadn't been born of parents. At slightest provocation, she would flinch and bristle and scurry away.

Lately Channing and Gary had been talking about finding her a car. Gary, always the hero. She would find those two with their heads together over eBay, talking high-mileage Bonnevilles or maybe an old Jetta or a truck. Thirty minutes later they'd be searching Corvettes, motorcycles made for off-road travel with horsepower off the charts, purple custom vans with flames on the side.

"Breakfast?" she asked, tossing the suggestion into thin air. "I've got—"

The door slammed. Billy returned and pressed his face flat against the screen. "McDonald's, Mom. Duh."

"Okay. McDonald's."

The most difficult part of today was pretending this was a regular trip, something they ought to look forward to. She grabbed a box of chocolate Pop-Tarts and handed them to Gary as he came downstairs, too, shrugging into his jacket.

He gripped the box inside one huge paw the same way he would grip a football. "What are these for?" He studied the label. Anything to keep his eyes averted from hers.

"For emergencies," she said. "In case one of us gets stranded on the road."

He studied his shoes.

"Do you have the map?" she asked. "The brochure?"

He placed his hand over the folded papers in his breast pocket. "Aubrey, listen. I—"

She touched his hand where it lay on his coat. "Let's just get on the road." When he moved his fingers, she rearranged the papers in his pocket to make certain the children wouldn't read anything revealing.

The center Gary had agreed to go to was one of the best private rehabs, everyone in the court system had told them. The judge had researched and approved it himself before the prosecutor would even agree to Gary traveling there. Aubrey had found the place herself, on the Internet and made the arrangements via the phone at odd hours when Hannah and Billy and Channing wouldn't overhear, talking to staff to be sure he could be admitted and that a bed was available, talking to the insurance company to see if they would pay.

In spite of the court documents being public record, Aubrey had vowed to protect the children from this. Her second priority had been to keep Gary's problem hidden from everyone. It seemed the worse thing she could think of, having people look at her and *know.*

My husband is an alcoholic.

"You ready to go?" Gary asked her now.

Aubrey nodded.

"Might as well get this show on the road."

"A circus," she commented without meeting his gaze. "Do you ever wonder where clichés come from? They were talking about a circus when they said that. 'Get this show on the road.'"

"That fits us," he said, a feeble attempt at joking. "Our lives are a circus."

She didn't smile.

"Kids!" Gary raised his voice. "Load up. Don't want to miss your plane."

"Did you get Hannah's suitcase? She carried it down for you."

He nodded. "Everything's in. Billy's already outside."

"You ready?" Aubrey asked Hannah. As she reached to scoop her littlest daughter into her arms, Channing grabbed Hannah instead and, in a sulk, bore her out the door.

Aubrey stared sadly after her oldest child, at the churlish set of her spine, the self-righteous way she tromped down the front steps. She said to her husband, "Channing doesn't want to be gone three weeks."

"She wouldn't have to be," Gary reminded her. "We don't have to ship them off to my sister's. We don't have to pretend that you and I are going off together."

"Of course we do."

"You could stay with them here while I'm in rehab."

"And just exactly what would I tell them? It's too much for them to have to deal with, Gary. It's too much for them to have to try to understand."

They'd come to the same stalemate at least a dozen times. Now that the children had gone ahead, the silence of the house seemed to wrap itself around them in censure.

My husband is an alcoholic.

"You're ashamed of me," he said.

"I'm not," she lied.

He gripped her shoulders. "Look at me, Aubrey. You haven't looked at me all morning."

"We're going to be late to the airport. Billy wants to stop by McDonald's."

"Look at me, Aubrey. Please."

Reluctantly, she raised her eyes to his. She saw her husband swallow in frustration, his Adam's apple move up and then down.

It doesn't matter what he thinks, she reminded herself. *I have every right to keep myself protected from more pain. Gary's drinking has hurt all of us.*

He'd left Billy at Carson Taylor's birthday party so late that Carson's mother had phoned to inform Aubrey that there must be some mistake, no one had come to pick up Billy, and he certainly hadn't been invited to a sleepover. He'd arrived at Channing's choir concert so drunk that he'd barely been able to stand. Aubrey lived in fear that Gary might drink too much and do some-

136

thing to hurt the baby. She counted it as a blessing that the police had picked him up while he staggered across the eleventh hole at Westmoreland Links in the dark, trying to find his way home.

"Please listen to me," he said now, and she could read the earnestness in his eyes as he clutched her shoulders. But Gary had been earnest before. "Don't you know that, if I could, I would do things differently?"

Aubrey steeled herself against his words. Gary never would have admitted that he had a problem, never would have even sought this treatment, if it hadn't been a court decree.

"I'd move the clock back if I could," he said, "but I can't. I can only go forward." Her husband stood over her, brooding, unable to say more. If this had been three months ago, if she had still been trying to read his emotions, she would have thought him bitter, nervous, embarrassed. But she knew better now. Emotions didn't rule her husband. His drinking did.

"We're going to be late to the airport," she said.

"You've closed yourself off from me, Aubrey," he said. "We'll never be able to salvage this if you aren't willing to give me another chance."

The afternoon Hunter and Sam reached Piddock Beach, it had begun to rain. As they'd driven toward the Washington border where the highway joined the Columbia River, the sky had turned as dark as smoke. By the time they reached The Dalles, where wagons had forded a hundred and fifty years ago, they found themselves inside a gorge, amidst forests of ancient juniper and hemlock.

The road dropped dramatically toward the Pacific Ocean. The shadows became deep and mossy and the air took on a chill. Hunter, who'd only worn a T-shirt and baggy shorts, dug in his duffel until he found a hooded sweatshirt to keep warm. As the river grew wider and they passed Multnomah Falls, rain plinked the leaves of the trees the way fingers plink piano keys. They drove past scenic turnoffs, and narrow passage-ways with arrows to wilderness areas, and a dam built with locks so the salmon could spawn upstream.

After they shot through Portland and headed north-west, the small blackberry farms and fruit stands emerged like watercolor blotches through the car's rain-streaked, fogged windows. Occasionally the foliage that crowded the two-lane road would break away to reveal a misted distance of green hills, a scat-tering of Holsteins grazing beside a barn. Then they came upon a weathered sign for the old Agate Shop, a roadside store that sold rocks from the beach and local crafts and cement birdbaths. Sam glanced across the front seat at his nephew.

"Well, buddy. Looks like we're almost there."

"That's what I was afraid of."

Which brought complete silence, except for Ginny's panting, in the car.

When they entered Piddock Beach, Sam did not try to appraise his rush of feeling. Everything here seemed so small through the blurred windows. Was that because he had been here when he was small so he remembered everything large? Or was it because the details of Piddock Beach had grown in his memory and now, seeing details in reality, he found them deflated?

"Right around this corner," Sam said, "is the taffy shop. Your mother ate so much taffy, I'm surprised she didn't lose all her teeth in there."

But the Seaside Salt Water Taffy Shoppe was no longer in business. Sam recognized the remains of the white stucco gas station on Main Street, its broad glass front shattered and crosshatched with tape, its sign broken out in chunks. Instead of the hodgepodge of shops and kites and wooden tables that had once lined the boardwalk, a strip of uniform signs now bordered the street. Gone were the elaborate parking meters at the curb and the steps that had led to the Scandinavian pastry shop and the place that had sold hand-blown fishing floats beside the pier. They passed acres and acres of outlet mall. Placards directed him to the nearest underground garage.

Nothing was as he'd remembered it. Sam knew without question where the motor court ought to be. But when he made the next turn, expecting a vast expanse of dunes and the Sunset Vue Motor Court to appear, he found high-rise condos blocking the view of the sea.

"How do you even *get* to it anymore?" Sam wondered.

"What?"

"The *water.*"

Hunter shrugged. "How am I supposed to know?"

Sam floored the accelerator and headed in the only other direction he knew to go. When he turned onto the street, the traffic was bumper to bumper. A dune buggy inched along in front of them, its pistons hammering discontent. Guiltily, he proceeded toward the McCarts' house, thinking he might as well get that disappointment out of the way, too.

The entrance to the neighborhood had been widened; they entered through a broad gate marked SANDVIEW POINT. Yes, there were tract houses here just as he'd expected, perfect lawns with flagstone walks snaking toward front doors and profusions of geraniums. But towering over the shingled roofs, Sam could still see grandfather evergreens growing. It gave him hope to see rooflines of older bungalows among the trees.

"Where are we?" Hunter said. "Why are we driving around looking at houses?"

Sam didn't answer immediately. There it was, number 503, the ample driveway curving past the myrtlewood tree. The paneled glass door was still intact, its wood painted Essex green. The porch, shielded on both sides by balusters, stood empty except for a weather-worn rocking chair, its seat unraveling. The Douglas fir had overgrown the curb and towered over the house. The rain had tinted its wooden façade a dark, unimpressive gray. Rust stains ran at regular intervals wherever there was a nail.

Nostalgia clogged Sam's throat. How many years had it been? And yet, it might as well have been yesterday.

You're a grown man, Sam, he lectured himself. *You're being ridiculous, imagining the past. How they'd laugh if they could read your mind. You're acting like more of a teenager than your nephew.*

"Why are you staring at that old place?" Hunter asked.

Sam could have simply told him the truth. He could have used such weightless, easy words, been so non-committal. *I had a best friend who lived here once. Did anyone ever tell you that?*

But just as he started to explain, the door opened and a stranger came out, some young, dark-haired woman with a baby. Well, what had he been thinking? Of course Aubrey didn't live here anymore.

He felt heat rising from his neck, felt the rims of his ears begin to burn. He murmured something to his nephew about getting lost, trying to find the beach. "Isn't that it down there?" Hunter pointed and, through the sweep of windshield wipers, Sam got his first glimpse in twenty years of the expanse of whitecaps, churning gray.

Sam could see a boat coming in, not doing too well negotiating the chop. He recognized off-shore rocks and roosting pelicans, shapes that had been lasered into his mind over the years. He understood, in that moment, the true meaning of timelessness. His mood lifted considerably. For the first time in days, he felt expectant. It didn't matter how people saw it now or thought Piddock Beach had changed. For Sam, the feeling of magic arrival would always stay the same.

141

• • •

"I wanted to go with you to see Grandpa living on his boat," Billy said, looking pitiful, his chin working against the top of the seat. "I don't know why we have to stay with Aunt Emily instead."

"Aunt Emily is taking you to Disneyland," Gary said as Aubrey gathered up napkins and ketchup packets. It hadn't taken long to demolish the fast food. "You'll have a much better time there."

"But I like the *boat*—"

"Your grandfather can only handle you for about two seconds. You'll be playing with your cousins. You can't complain about that."

Hannah wailed from behind them, "*Dad.* I forgot Elephant. We have to go *home.*"

Aubrey and Gary exchanged glances. They were in it now. Aubrey explained as well as she could. "We're too far away to go home, honey."

"But we *have* to. *Elephant's* there."

"We've gone too many miles, Hannah. We can't go back."

"Elephant will be lonely. *Dad.*"

"No, Hannah." And from Gary, amazing though it was, that was enough. Could a preschooler sense desperation in her father's voice even though she couldn't hear it?

The windows had fogged up because of the rain. Or maybe, Aubrey thought, it was from the internal combustion of everyone inside. Channing stayed as far away from the rest of them as she could manage, sprawled across the width of the SUV on seats that could also be folded up for luggage, her mukluks crossed at the ankles, propped against the door.

Aubrey didn't know how the children hadn't noticed the changes in Gary. Mercifully, no one in the expensive private school they attended had seen fit to discuss the police reports that ran sporadically on the local page. But the lines on her husband's face told the story itself—his pale square cheeks that looked the consistency of bread dough, the wrinkles that had seeped in around his eyes, hair that had turned brittle gray, as if Gary had walked through colorless clouds of ash. He'd grown more tired, older. Broken that fast. Almost overnight.

They began to see signs for Portland International Airport and Gary worked his way into the correct lane. Security made it so difficult these days. They would have to find a place to park, check the children in, and only one of them would have a receipt to escort the little ones through screening.

The other would have to say good-bye at the counter.

She laid a hand on Gary's knee as if she were doing him a favor. "I'll take them through," she volunteered.

When his chin shot up, she knew he saw through it. He glanced across the front seat and she knew he understood. If she left him alone with them, she was afraid of what he might say.

Billy began to complain again. "I *don't* know why you and Dad think it's so important to go away *alone*." From the sound of his voice, Aubrey knew they blamed this fiasco on her. They all knew she could convince Gary to do what she wanted.

"Sometimes parents need to go away—" *They need to go away from each other,* she might have said.

She and the kids made it through security with a great thumping of tubs, the removal of shoes and boots—Billy's sneakers scattering dirt all over the belt when he took them off—a long second look at Channing's bottomless leather bag, and Hannah's blanket having to be removed from her clutches so it could be scanned. As Aubrey noted the lumbering aircraft outside, one of which would take her children away, it seemed ridiculous that such things could fly.

When they arrived at the gate, the plane had begun boarding. Aubrey introduced her brood to the ticket agent and handed over the documents that enabled children to travel alone. Now that the moment had come and everything had been set into motion, Aubrey felt a hollow sensation that she almost couldn't bear. "Hey," she reminded them, holding her arms out when they began to walk directly toward the door. "Don't I get a hug or something?"

Billy was the only one who came back. Channing had already turned her earphones on and Hannah only looked wistful. She'd reverted; her thumb was in her mouth as her big sister dragged her along by the hand.

"See you, Mom." Billy's words were offhanded, his lips wet and cool. She didn't dare keep him longer with the girls gone on ahead.

"See you, little man."

As Aubrey watched his compact little shoulders retreating, it seemed like her entire life had walked away.

Chapter Fourteen

Sam felt the shock of recognition the instant he noticed the photograph on the wall at the Sea Basket. While he and Hunter stood in line for a table, he took a quick look around, found himself staring at a likeness of an old friend.

A faded picture of a young soldier wearing his dress uniform, the stripe of a private on his sleeve, before he'd made it to first class. Sam didn't have to look twice to be sure. The boy's smile was evident in his eyes even though his lips were pressed into a menacing scowl. Someone must have coached him to appear intimidating in uniform.

OUR FALLEN SON, the plaque read. KENNETH MCCART. KILLED IN ACTION DECEMBER 1970.

Sam felt raw close to his chest. Kenneth had been so sure that he could find his own way. Make it back.

Hunter was looking at him, his hands shoved inside the pockets of his baggy shorts. "Are you okay?"

The hostess must have found them a table. "This way, please." She carried menus in her hand.

"You know those people? The McCarts?" Sam asked the waitress, gesturing toward the photo before she led them away. "I did. A long time ago."

"Sorry." She shot him an apologetic smile. "Guess it was before my time."

Sam wondered if anyone noticed Kenneth's picture anymore, if anyone stopped to take a measure of the hope in the young man's eyes or to read the defiance in the cagey twist of his lips. At least the picture hadn't been thrown away; someone in Piddock Beach must remember Kenneth's name. Or maybe it was just another of those things that had become invisible.

Ten minutes later, Sam sat alone at the table, talking on his cell phone to Brenda, using a finger to bend the flap of his other ear. "You're not going to believe where I am," he yelled into the phone. "I'm at Sea Basket Steamer's. Remember po'boy sandwiches? . . . I know. Can you believe it's still here?"

His sister's voice was a thread connecting him to another life, so thin it might have never existed at all, transparent as a spider's web. With one swipe of hand, one brush through the air, their connection might be broken. He'd called her because he was excited. He couldn't say why her voice disappointed him now.

"It's the same. People still sit together even though they don't know each other. The waitress walks around with the basket of hot hush puppies." He was sure Brenda would laugh at that. Their parents had once broken up their hush puppy fights (Brenda always started those; Sam always got into trouble). The neon signs still shone a strong, fierce green, yellow, and red behind the bar. Fishing floats dangled overhead, cradled in dusty nets.

146

"You've got to let Dad know this place is still around, okay? I called but he doesn't answer . . . At the nursing home, right. Dad will get such a kick out of it. And maybe if he mentions it to Mom . . . The newspaper's still called the *Lighthouse-Reporter*."

Brenda began to ask questions on the other end of the line and Sam did his best to answer her. "Everything's good with Hunter," he lied. "We're getting along fine . . . Yes. Yes, we *have* been talking," as if he could count the dozen or so lines they'd exchanged.

When she asked if she could speak to her son, he felt like a cornered animal. "He's not with me right now. He's out walking the pier, getting the feel of the place." The rain had tapered off, leaving only rivulets of water rushing along the curb, wet pockmarks in the sand. "You know how it is here."

"I thought we could just go to McDonald's," Hunter had said the moment he saw they'd be sitting with strangers. "I don't want to sit with people I don't know."

"You need to try this," Sam insisted. "I don't care if you walk the pier until the chowder comes, but I'm going to make you try this."

"Hey," Sam said now, leaning slightly over the table. "I have to let you go. The food's coming." Then, "He'll be back any minute. Don't worry, Bren. I'm feeding him." And, "I don't have a number yet. We'll call tomorrow after we've gotten settled. How's that sound?"

She'd broken through a boundary again, pushing her

present concerns on him when he'd needed to share the memory of this place with her. He'd wanted her to be excited about his impressions of Piddock Beach. His sister was the only one who he had thought would understand. But instead he was saying, "Everything's going to be okay, Brenda. Hunter's fine. Really, you can stop asking that . . . Yes. Tomorrow. Fine. That will be fine." Then one last time to make sure she understood him, *"Fine."*

With a tap of his finger, he cut off the phone.

"You sat there beside me," Gary told Aubrey just before they parted, "acting like you were protecting them from something horrible."

"Who?" She feigned innocence.

"The kids. *Our* kids."

"I don't know what you're talking about." The rain had cleared, but the woodland around them was still dripping. A mist had settled low against the land, fog sieving through gaps between the wet trees.

In another life Aubrey would have stepped closer to her husband and straightened his jacket collar. She would have lifted her face to him and remained that way until he reached toward her and drew her against his chest. But she would do none of those things now.

Aubrey mouthed it quietly; maybe she hoped he wouldn't hear. "I was protecting them from the truth."

"Aubrey, I'm their *father.*"

"That's exactly the point."

A fancy scrollwork sign in blue, with gold letters that

148

said simply CRESTOVER TREATMENT CENTER, had directed them inside. After giving their names at a checkpoint, they traveled another mile along a narrow lane before they reached the main buildings. On the outside, the stone building looked serene and beautiful; it might have been a spa or a retreat instead of a medical facility. An attached wing elbowed to the north, another to the south. Water dashed over the scallops of a stone fountain, three tiers high.

Gary unloaded his small black suitcase from the SUV and they stood beside it for a long minute. They both took a deep breath at the same time. He scrubbed back his hair, revealing the gold glint of watchband at his wrist. Aubrey wrapped her arms around herself, feeling cold to her very bones, so cold that she didn't think she'd ever feel warm again.

"How many times are you going to make me pay for this?" he asked.

"Until it's over," she answered.

Aubrey had been wrong when she guessed that the drive with the children would be the worst part. This was more difficult by far. They were alone together and the truth could be discussed between them. Pretending for the children's sake had given them some degree of safety.

Now, that safety was gone. In a mirror motion to one he might have once expected from his wife, Gary took the corners of his collar between his fingers, pressed hard as if they'd told him to leave thumbprints. He craned his neck forward and straightened his collar himself, giving it sharp little yanks with each word. "I guess this is it."

"Yes."

"I don't want you to come inside with me."

She looked past him at the sizeable front door. "Are you sure?"

"Yes." He gripped the handle of his bag and lifted it. "How long did you say you'd be in Piddock Beach?"

"Two weeks, at least. I've rented the cottage for that length of time. After that, I don't know." Then, "Gary, don't rush this, for either of us. I want you to stay here as long as it takes."

"Do you?"

"Yes."

"Or are you not sure whether or not you want me to come home at all?"

Her eyes shot toward his. *Was* that her motive? Was Gary reading her, or merely trying to make her afraid? "That isn't fair, Gary, saying that now. When we're about to part."

"We won't be talking by phone. They've said they won't let me do that. We'll be cut off—"

"All the same, we won't make assumptions today. It's too soon." At that moment, even the thought of letting him walk through the treatment-center door by himself terrified her.

She guessed that he must have read it in her face. "You going to be okay?"

"Yes." And the rest went unsaid. *I'm much better off now I know you'll be taken care of.*

Gary didn't move for a minute. Two minutes. He stood there in front of her, clutching his suitcase handle in both hands. The mist had thickened, enclosing them in an ever-dwindling circle. They were socked in. Somewhere in the distance, an osprey shrieked and its cry seemed muffled by the fog. Gary readjusted his grip on the suitcase. "I know I've hurt you, Aubrey. I know I'm not the man you married." He surveyed the mist somewhere past her left shoulder, his lips set in a grim line.

It was the perfect moment to encourage him, to say, *Of course you are, Gary. You need to get well, is all. And I know you can do it for us.* But Aubrey didn't say those things.

She had expected him to succeed in this battle so many times before. She'd had so much faith in him once. He'd guaranteed her that he'd change, and she'd applauded every time he promised to throw out his bottles and stop spending long hours at the clubhouse bar.

Then, every time, he started drinking again and dashed her hopes.

Aubrey just couldn't get her hopes up anymore. She felt numb and cold and empty, especially with the children gone.

Gary started toward the entryway, stopped, turned as if to catch one final glimpse of her. "You take care," he mouthed across the way. He lifted his fingers, curled slightly, in half salute, half wave.

He's my husband. I should be sad that we're parting. But I'm not.

Aubrey stood hugging herself, feeling nothing. She didn't wave back.

CHAPTER FIFTEEN

Aubrey unlocked the door to the little cottage room she had rented and fumbled along the wall until she found the light switch. When the light came on, she discovered a swaybacked bed and a television with the channel directory fixed to its top. Off to the right, a Formica-covered counter, a row of cabinets, and a two-burner stove constituted a kitchen. She dropped her room-key card on the dresser beside the plastic ice bucket.

The place was chilly and cramped and smelled of mildew. Aubrey plopped her bag on the floor and turned up the heat. Then she stood in the middle of the room, rubbing her hands along her arms to warm herself, wondering what she ought to do with herself.

Her dad would have long been asleep on his boat by now. She teased him for still keeping fisherman's hours, "Up with the sun, out with the tide, roost with the seagulls," she liked to say, hoping he would smile. After all these years, she still tried to invoke the humor he kept so carefully guarded. Her father had stopped laughing when his son died.

Aubrey thought about phoning Emily to make sure the kids had arrived safely. When she checked her watch, she guessed they'd be in Emily's Suburban headed toward Lancaster. If they asked to speak to

Gary, she wouldn't know what to tell them.

Already, she would be caught in deception.

She hadn't moved from the center of the room. She hugged her arms again and stared at the empty wall. Loneliness washed over her with such force that it made her feel faint.

What would she do all this time without the kids?

Aubrey had often lamented how their activity never ceased around her. She always felt a step behind as the days kept shooting past. *Just once, I'd like to finish a thought,* she'd bemoaned. *I'd like to spend just one day when life didn't feel like a whirlwind around me.*

She'd forgotten that she existed for any purpose other than raising her children, keeping them safe.

If I could ever get away by myself, I'd come back as good as new.

Here she was, finally alone, missing them beyond measure.

A heavy curtain hung in folds beyond the edge of the bed. Aubrey stepped forward with resolve and swept it aside. When it swung open, it revealed a sliding door and, beyond that, a patio bordering the dunegrass. Aubrey unfastened the lock, stood a moment with her splayed fingers smudging the glass.

Aubrey trained her ears. She could hear the waves even through the door. They were breaking farther out, just beyond the jetty. It must be slack tide. The spit would be above water tonight and a gathering of harbor seals would be lolling in the sand. She wondered what it would feel like to go clamming again, to have the cries of the gulls awaken her in the morning.

Maybe she'd drive over to the pier tomorrow and buy a shovel.

At last, she threw open her patio door and took a deep draught of salt air. She stood with her eyes closed, loving the scent and the gentle rolling of the water. She realized now, for the first time in days, that she felt like she could breathe.

With his hands shoved in his pockets, Sam picked his way through clumps of dunegrass toward the shore. The rental he'd found for them was adequate, nothing special, but it had a separate bed for him and Hunter, and the price hadn't been bad. Hotels with NO VACANCY signs had sprung up everywhere.

Sam counted himself lucky to have found anything on the beach.

The way to the water was tricky from here, following faint trails through hedges of salal and the fragrant wild roses, down a steep bank of round stones worn smooth as pottery by the waves. He stepped over stacks of driftwood and tangles of kelp in the darkness, finally found the sand. He stopped there, rubbing the back of his neck as he gazed into a sky that had almost cleared, which boded well for the weather tomorrow. Only a few tattered clouds remained, fraying as they moved across the moon.

As the stars began to come out, they reminded him of an earlier conversation with Kil. "Don't tell me you believe in eternity," the man who had begun to signify so much to Sam had said. They'd taken a seat on a narrow curb one night near Kil's lean-to that doubled as his sleeping quarters.

"Yes," Sam had answered, cupping his knees with his hands as if to stand. "I do."

"The way I see it, preacher man, that makes you crazier than me."

"You want to see it?"

"Say what? You got it in your pocket or something?"

"Look up," Sam remembered saying. They both lifted their eyes to the sky. "What do you see there?"

Kil, with his back braced against the brick wall, had only grunted.

"Where does that end?"

"Got to end somewhere, preacher man."

"If it ends somewhere, then what's on the other side?"

As Sam stood remembering, thoughts of his congregation in Des Moines began to roll over him in pace with the rumble of the waves. Lester Kraft and his tendency toward scientific debate. Dottie Graham and her excitement over the care packages she'd sent for her son to share in the Army hospital. Grant Ransom and the confidences they'd shared. Sam ached at this loss. No matter what had gone between him and Grant, Sam missed talking with his friend.

It hit Sam suddenly that it wasn't the day-to-day responsibilities of Covenant Heights he missed. It was the faces of those he loved. He toyed with worry, did not let it overtake him.

He'd asked questions of himself, and found he could

be willing to accept what the Father had for him.

It wasn't the staff meetings or the decision-making or the way some held him in esteem at Covenant Heights that he pined for. It was being a part of Lester, and Dottie and Grant and everyone else's everyday lives. It was watching their faith growing through their own eyes, the stories they imparted to him, this was the treasure.

Father, if someone besides me could pastor them better, pray better, lead them better than I can, help me to see it. Help me to love them enough to want that for them.

If he'd thought there had been a magnitude of stars visible before, he looked now and saw the sky on an unfathomable scale. It had been years since he'd surveyed the heavens away from city lights. No doubt Lester could have discussed this completely. So many sources of light spread across millions of miles, so far away that years passed before they became visible. Between every star, Sam could see another.

I'll rest, if you want, Lord. I surrender my exhaustion to you. Only, show me how to be open to what you want from me here.

A clicking of stones behind him told him he was no longer alone. Sam turned, saw a silhouette picking its way along the driftwood. A string of porch lights from the cottages backlit his visitor. Even shading his eyes with his hand, Sam could not see.

"How come you're standing out here?"

"Hunter."

"You've been gone a long time."

"Just trying to soak up the ocean."

"Oh."

Hunter's jacket was flailing in the wind. He turned to look at the waves, too. "You really like it here, don't you?"

"Yeah, I do."

The water slipped in scallops toward their feet. Hunter stepped toward the sea, as if his proximity to it would help him understand its odd allure to his uncle. Against the white arcs of the breakers, Sam could read the sullen slope of the boy's shoulders, the angry slant of his forearms. Sam lifted a hand toward Hunter, reaching to clasp his shoulder, the bittersweet tenderness he'd found for his church flock transferring itself completely to this boy.

But something stopped him from touching his nephew.

Father, I don't want to offer anything to Hunter that isn't real. He knows me at my worst. He'll see through anything I try to do if I'm not sincere.

Sam's fingers curled, uncurled, did not find their mark. His hand fell to his side.

Somewhere in the distance a boat sounded its horn, mournful and deep. A spear of light from the Tillamook Head Lighthouse sliced across the water and played along the edges of the off-shore rocks.

"I want you to know that you were right about me," Sam said to his nephew's back.

The boy did not move. Sam waited, his eyes trained

on the contour of Hunter's hair where it came to a shaggy edge at the nape of his neck.

"You were right, what you said to me in the car. About the things you overheard me say to your mother. I told her I wouldn't consider spending time with you."

Slack tide must be almost over. The surf slid onto the sand and threatened the boy's feet.

"The most important thing is for you and me to be honest with each other."

Hunter zipped his jacket completely to his neck.

"Your mother thinks I'm the one with all the answers. She's always been wrong about that."

The boy finally turned. When he spoke, his words were almost lost in the tumble of the waves.

"You loved my father, too, didn't you?"

And Sam nodded. "Yes. I did."

Aubrey watched the beam from the Tillamook Head Lighthouse sweep in a diligent circle across the bay. She twisted her set of wedding rings—the half-carat solitaire set in yellow gold, the matching narrow gold band—around and around the finger on her left hand. When she removed them with one easy tug and left them lying in her lap, Aubrey wasn't sure exactly why she did so.

It wasn't that she didn't want to be married to Gary anymore. It was just that being married to *anyone* seemed a lot of trouble. It seemed fair somehow, a sort of trade for the nights she'd lain awake wishing he would come home or for the police call about the bel-

158

ligerent way he'd tried to slug them on the golf green or for the brave face she wore at the supper table for the children.

She took off the ring because she wanted to walk around unfettered, unlabeled. She didn't want to be prodded right now, or made to bristle, or even made to move.

Long ago, in the first month they'd been married probably, she'd had the rings welded together. Now Aubrey bore them inside the cottage, carrying them between her thumb and her forefinger, aloft and aware, the same way she'd carry a lit match. She found a box of foil in the little kitchenette. She ripped off a sliver, made a small case out of it, and tucked the rings inside.

She'd read on the Internet how the packet would be perfectly protected on the bottom shelf of the freezer. She placed the packet there, exactly as specified. She straightened her spine in victory, closed the refrigerator door, and returned to the patio.

There were people from the cottages standing by the water. She could hear male voices conversing. Although she tried to eavesdrop, she couldn't make out their words as she stood squeezing her own bare hand, awash in guilt, feeling keenly that something was missing.

Was it wrong to miss her husband with this longing, and wish herself free of him, too?

Aubrey reminded herself that Gary had made his own choices. She reminded herself that she didn't care.

• • •

Hunter and Sam trekked together along the pier early the next morning and, although Hunter still walked three steps ahead of his uncle with his fists shoved inside his jacket pockets, he approached the morning with an air of acceptance. When Sam stopped to watch a crab boat pulling up its pots, Hunter stopped to watch, too. When Sam pointed out how the seagulls followed the crabbers, swirling overhead, their white tails flashing in the sun, Hunter observed the scene with slight interest. When Sam stopped to inquire of a weather-worn fisherman on the pier, "How's the fishing going today?" and the man replied, "Fishing's great, it's the catching that's bad," Hunter joined in the genial laughter.

It doesn't take long on a pier to convince a man and a boy to hurry to a supply shop to purchase licenses and buckets and bait. "You ready to try your hand at this, too?" Sam asked, straightening from where he was standing at the railing.

Hunter looked thoughtful for a moment. Then, "Well, I guess so."

When Sam pushed open the door to Piddock Beach Sporting Goods ten minutes later, an overhead bell heralded their arrival. It took Sam a few moments to get his bearing, so great was the clutter. Rows upon rows of sea kayaks dangled from the ceiling. Aluminum-handled fishing nets stood in barrels, arranged like giant bouquets. A queue of yellow squall hats stood next to an array of jelly-like jigging baits in brilliant oranges and greens and pinks.

Sam picked up a tide table, a booklet provided by the shop, informing beachgoers of the time and measure of high tides and low tides, every day.

They spent longer than they'd planned stocking up with supplies, one surf-casting rod that they'd agreed to share, a bucket, a plastic shellfish gauge, two tiny bait baskets to entice Dungeness crabs onto the sand, and a cardboard package of frozen squid. When it came their turn at the checkout stand, Sam slid their selected items toward the cash register. "Oh, and one more thing I almost forgot. We've got to have a clam shovel. I never did find one anywhere."

"Afraid you're out of luck on the clam shovel, mister. Some lady come in and bought our last one, not more'n an hour ago."

Aubrey spent her day in Piddock Beach idly beach combing and exploring the tide pools she'd loved so much as a child. She speared the sand in likely places with her new clam shovel, and when she came up empty-handed every time, decided that she must have lost her touch.

Aubrey took a short drive south mid-afternoon to Cape Kiwanda. She stopped at the Sea Basket on her way home and, in a great surge of nostalgia as she stood before her brother's photograph, ordered a large green salad and hush puppies and a bowl of clam chowder to go. She ate her supper alone, sitting on the stoop of her open sliding door, vaguely aware of someone sitting a few patios over. She'd noticed them when she'd come in—a man and his teenaged son. Now there was a blaring television and some sort of hairy, big dog.

When Aubrey stepped inside to discard her plastic salad bowl and the thin, disposable fork, she heard the guest down the way begin to strum his guitar. For long moments she listened, not understanding the music her neighbor was playing. It wasn't a song exactly, just a formation of chords, an organic melody in which each note trended toward the next before it arrived.

Then she understood; he was composing. It was quite a nice tune, actually.

She returned to her door to hear more. She happened to glance in his direction at the same instant he rose and turned on the porch light against the oncoming dusk. He stood peering into his window and his features, made bright by the light from inside, were familiar. Aubrey let her breath out slowly. Her ears began to ring at the sight of his face.

It wasn't possible. Not possible that she would happen to look up and he would be here after all these years.

But then, yes. Sam Tibbits had always come here, too. They had *met* each other here. *It must* be possible.

She felt like she'd traveled back years in time. A childhood heart never forgets. He had been the only friend she'd ever had who she trusted enough to talk about everything.

If I say something and it isn't him, he'll think I'm an idiot.

162

When Sam Tibbits had kissed her the first time on the beach, her chest had constricted and her stomach had turned somersaults and she hadn't been able to stop smiling for weeks.

If I don't say something and it is *Sam, I will have missed my chance.*

When she stood, her knees were wobbly. She placed her hand over her heart because it felt like it might fly out of her chest. She counted each step as she crossed the grass.

He turned from the window, picked up his guitar, and laid it against his lap. She hoped he wouldn't stop messing around with it. The music had been nice. That was the thing that confused her, though; Sam had never played the guitar. She waited in full view, staring at him, thinking, *If he recognizes me, he'll say something.*

"Nice night," she commented.

"Sure is," he said.

Oh, this is ridiculous. It's been too many years. It can't be him! Besides, he'd look different by now, wouldn't he?

The kitchen light flooded out the window, formed a pool on the bug-encrusted fender of his car. In that pool of yellow, she saw the license plate, IOWA. That license plate made her brave enough to stay rooted to the spot.

"Excuse me," she said to him. "You might think I'm crazy . . . It's probably because I'm in this place on vacation, reminiscing, but you look familiar. You look like somebody I used to know."

He stared at her, his eyes perplexed, his mouth in a

quizzical smile. His hair was darker than she remembered. That's when she noticed his hands still resting on the strings, his fingers broad and strong. His nails were as square as Chiclets. And she thought, *I will never forget those hands as long as I live.*

She cocked her chin at him, tried to think of something she used to say. "Did you know that a crocodile can't stick out its tongue? Or that a snail can sleep for three years?"

Without taking his eyes from her, he laid the guitar aside. "Aubrey? Oh my word, *Aubrey?* Don't tell me it's *you!*"

She nodded.

He sprang from the chair, jumped off the patio in an instant, and hauled her into an embrace. His guitar fell over and made a hollow clatter on the deck. Sam didn't notice. He held her at arm's length and examined her face.

Questions began flying, piling up one on top of the other, from both directions at once. "What are you doing here?" "How long has it been?" "What have you been up to?" "How have you been?" "It's crazy, isn't it?" "I thought it was you!"

They drew slightly away, stood clasping each other's elbows, studying each other's faces. Sam's eyes had narrowed with mirth. Aubrey shook her head with joy. "We're both talking at once," she said. They started laughing at each other and couldn't stop.

All those questions they'd asked, and neither had answered a word!

"You look *good,* Aubrey," he told her.

She wrenched one arm away from his and smoothed her hair, suddenly conscious of how she must appear. She wasn't old exactly, but she wasn't young anymore, either. Of course, she'd added a few telltale pounds. The years she'd spent in the sun on her father's fishing boats could be read in spots that passed as freckles, but were not.

But none of it mattered, she realized as she tucked a strand of hair behind one ear. What difference did it make? She didn't look at him and see a grown-up. She saw a boy, and his smile made her fourteen again.

"So do you," she said, and meant it. "Sam, you look good, too."

"Thanks," he said, still studying her. "Wow."

"I agree. Wow."

"Oh, man," he said, his eyes still bright. "Where did you come from? Aubrey, do you *live* here?"

"No, I don't. Not anymore."

"Well, then—"

"I'm staying in one of the units." She pointed. "Three doors down."

His gaze followed her gesture. "I can't believe it."

"I know."

"Wow."

"I know."

They'd run out of words. The joy of recognition slowly mellowed, followed by an awkward pause that neither knew how to breech. Dunegrass rustled at their feet.

She stepped backward and straightened her sleeves.

He smiled at her and had no idea what else to say.

"If you don't live here," he asked at last, "then what are you doing?"

"I'm just . . ." She stopped, knowing that now wasn't the time to tell him the truth; to do so would seem a betrayal to Gary. Sam had been someone she'd trusted years ago. He was a stranger now.

"I'm just traveling through."

"I see."

"How about you?"

She saw a shadow cross his face but, before she could read it, the expression was gone. "Same thing as you."

"Traveling through?"

"Yeah."

"Hmmm."

"How long will you be around?" he asked.

She voiced the stunning thought—"I've got reservations for two weeks. Only, it could be longer"—before her heart seized. Was that saying too much?

He seemed to sense, as he'd often sensed when they were young, that she needed a route of escape. Which he gave her by diversion.

"Hey. You got a minute? You have to hurry off or anything?"

"Nope. Don't have to hurry. Don't have anywhere else to go right now."

"I seem to remember a girl who was the best clam digger in all of Tillamook County. She taught me everything I knew."

"Well, not anymore, Sam. You should have seen how I did today."

"Today?"

"Yeah."

"You went clamming today?"

"I bought a clam shovel and went out—"

"You bought a shovel today?"

"—It was so bad. I don't know what was wrong. I kept digging the right places—"

"You're the *one*. Shame on you."

"I'm the one, what?"

"You bought the last clam shovel before we had a chance to get it. *You*." He reached over and goosed her in the ribs the way he'd done what seemed a lifetime ago.

She doubled up. She knew exactly how to protect herself. "Stop it."

"I'm going to have to take your new shovel and teach you a lesson or two. I'll bet I'm better at digging clams than you are."

"You are not." She reached over and goosed him back. And suddenly they were laughing again, the untroubled laughter of the young, innocent and pure, as sparkling as the droplets that flew toward the sun when a wave crashed onto shore.

The laughter went deeper, lasted longer this time, before wariness overtook them again. When words left them, Sam sat down on the edge of the patio, scrutinizing her up and down, making her slightly uneasy. "You were a silhouette at first. If not, I would have known you. You're just the same. You have the same smile, the same expression in your eyes."

That was nice. "You think so?"

"Absolutely." Then, "I shouldn't tell you this, should I? I drove past your old house the other day. Did you know that?" he asked as an electric zing shot through her. "First thing I did when I came into town."

She felt too breathless to laugh.

"I did."

"You're crazy, Sam Tibbits."

"That's not the first time you've said that to me, Aubrey. But look now. Here you *are*."

"Did you ever tell your parents that it wasn't you who got those clams that night?"

He beckoned her toward the stoop, that old glint of challenge in his eyes. "Why should I risk my reputation like that? Of course I didn't tell."

She couldn't stop herself from asking, "You haven't forgotten any of it, have you?"

"No, Aubrey. I haven't."

Suddenly, he found something interesting beyond the toe of his right shoe. She sat on a step, propped her elbow on her knee, her chin in her palm. He reached behind her for the guitar and fingered a B-minor. She arched her neck and examined the stars.

He strummed the chord. "I mean, it all comes back, you know?"

And she said quietly, "I know."

"We ought to go out to dinner and really catch up, find out what each other have been doing. What do you think about that?"

"We could," she said tentatively, "since we're both here."

Sam began to pick a tune, to tap the rhythm with his foot, and she listened a while. She scratched her arm and was glad there weren't mosquitoes this close to the water. The ocean breeze kept them away.

"I didn't know you played the guitar."

"I didn't." He turned a screw, strummed the same chord as if he heard a note that dissatisfied him.

"I like it. That's what made me notice you down here."

"That came . . ." But he hesitated, seemed to rethink what he'd been about to say. ". . . later. That came later in my life."

Later in my life. A sudden sense of loss blindsided her. She grieved for the snapshots of his life which she would never see, scenes she'd thought, when she'd been young, that she stood a chance of playing a role in.

"So what do you do," she asked, "for a job?"

When he hesitated, it was clear to her that he didn't want to say.

"Is it that funny? Is it that bad?"

"I'm a minister," he answered.

She threw back her head and lost it, her mirth pealing sharp and pure into the night. Her heart had ricocheted from one thing to another in these past few minutes, and now this.

"Don't laugh."

"A minister? Of a church?"

"I used to talk about it some."

"You did? Never with me. You never said anything about that to me."

"I'm a man of God who likes to dig clams. What's so funny about that?"

"You don't look like a preacher."

"Oh, really. What's a preacher supposed to look like then?"

"Oh, *you* know. A dark suit tailored at the hips with a flashy tie. The hair slicked back with pomade. The jowls that jiggle when you say–" She acted it out, lowering her voice for him, raising her hands. "—'Praise the Lord!' "

"I'm working on the jowls. It's taking time and a lot of cheesecakes."

The snapshots I missed aren't what I expected.

"So, whatever happened to old Mox?"

"Little Mox. Poor Moxie." To her horror she began to cry. From laughter to tears in, what, something like fifteen seconds? Her emotions sprang dangerously close to the surface. "He died." She touched the corners of her eyes with her fingers, trying to regain her composure.

"I never should have asked that question right now. Something that I already knew would have a sad ending. Of course Mox died. If he hadn't he'd be, oh, how many years old by now?"

"Don't count the years," she shrieked. "Whatever you do, don't count the years. Especially not *dog* years."

"I'm sorry."

"He got hit by a car."

"I shouldn't have brought it up."

The teenager he'd come with was inside his cottage and the television was still going strong. "I think it would really work, going out to dinner," Sam said, glancing toward the door. "I don't think my nephew would mind."

It was ridiculous, but she caught herself thinking, *Oh, he's a nephew. He isn't a son.*

Aubrey glanced at Sam's left hand, looking for the telltale gold band, and grew flustered when his eyes followed hers. She couldn't recall ever glancing at a man's hand before. She hadn't wanted him to see her checking. She hadn't noticed him checking hers. And that was good because it felt safer. Maybe he didn't care.

She didn't know what sort of church he was the pastor of. Maybe he *couldn't.*

He wore no ring. But then, neither did she.

"No, he isn't my son."

"Oh."

Then, in an old-fashioned way, as if the two facts could be connected in some way anymore, "I'm not married."

"Oh." And she didn't know why she felt relieved at that. She didn't know why it felt like a gift for tonight, except that she'd just found him again and she didn't want to have to share him with anyone.

"If you don't want to leave him—"

"It was my idea, wasn't it?"

"Yes."

"Well, let's do it."

"It's late, Sam. I ought to let you go."

"I'll talk to him. We can hang out tomorrow. Just someplace simple where we can talk. Maybe the Sea Basket—"

"No. Not the Sea Basket. I'd like to go somewhere else."

"Tomorrow then. I'll come knock," and his voice seemed to transport itself over years.

"Tomorrow," she said.

"It's good to see you," he said.

After she traversed the grass to her own patio, she stood there for a long time, her back braced against the clapboards, before she heard the gentle closing of his door.

CHAPTER SIXTEEN

Sam awakened the next day to a soft fog out the window, a gray as soft as a dove's wing. Mist hugged the seacoast every morning; it would burn off by eleven o'clock.

From his vantage point, Sam could see Hunter's nose still burrowed against the pillow in the bed next to his, his hair poking in a dozen different directions. Hunter was snoring slightly. His lips, thick with sleep, hung open at the same angle as a halibut's.

Seeing Aubrey the night before might have been a dream.

If the rental had a kitchen, Sam would have fixed breakfast. He would have snuck into the market while Hunter slept and bought pancake mix and butter and maple syrup. He would have fried them fluffy on the inside, crisp and brown on the outside. His nephew would have awakened to the mouth-watering smell.

Sam was hungry enough to eat a bear!

Hunter had stayed up late last night watching TV. He would sleep for at least another hour. In haste, Sam shoved back the covers and headed for the shower. After he'd dressed, towel-dried his hair, and left Hunter a note as to his whereabouts, Sam tiptoed out the door and latched it quietly behind him. He took his car through the nearest carwash. He found a bakery with a sign that advertised "hearty breakfasts."

That fit the bill. Sam walked inside to lights and morning chatter and the steaming cappuccino machine. Mountains of flaky croissants and fresh-baked pastries waited inside polished glass cases. He ordered eggs and bacon, and then pointed out to the hostess which baked goods he'd like. Yes, he was selecting more than he needed, but who cared! They looked so good that he couldn't decide.

It seemed his senses had sprung to life. When had he last looked forward to something? Sam found a table in the shade along the sidewalk where he sipped the most robust, fragrant coffee of his life. When the waitress brought his meal, he lowered his head and thanked his heavenly Father. When he began to eat, the bacon crunched against his tongue and tasted of hickory. He dug into the crisp, white sack and slathered a croissant with butter and strawberry jam. He sank his teeth in, closing his eyes in bliss.

I saw Aubrey last night, and I'm going to see her again tonight. We're going to catch up.

The thought felt laden with possibility and bottom-less. Sam's stomach filled with apprehension. His fork paused in mid-air. He stared at his half-eaten eggs and realized that he'd been insane to order all this food.

He wasn't hungry anymore.

When Sam returned to their rented room, he found Hunter's bed empty and the shower running. Sam unloaded the goodies he'd bought, laying them out on the bureau like treasure, a quart of cold milk and the pastries, a raspberry turnover, a blueberry Danish, and a sticky bun. When Hunter turned off the water, Sam knocked. "Hey, you sleepyhead. There's food out here."

The fog outside had begun to dissipate, not fading away exactly, but interspersing with strands of blue. Sam couldn't stop himself from glancing toward the sliding door, the patio. Would Aubrey be sitting there? Or would she be running around Piddock Beach, doing the things he'd expect her to be doing, shopping along Main Street and seeing old haunts, digging clams, vis-iting friends? He didn't know. He *wanted* to know.

What could she be doing this minute?

Hunter appeared behind him. "Where did that come from?"

"What, the pastries? I bought them. Some bakery down the street."

"No. Not the pastries." Hunter pointed toward the glass. It was the first time that Sam noticed the clam shovel propped against the door. "I'm talking about *that*."

"Oh," Sam said. *Oh.* Then, "I can't imagine."

But, of course, he knew. After hesitating a little, he said, "Aubrey must have brought it over."

"Aubrey?"

"Aubrey—" Sam realized he had no idea what her last name might be.

"The lady you were talking to last night?"

"Yes."

"Who is she, anyway?"

"An old friend."

There was a silent moment which begged to be filled with explanation. Sam didn't choose to fill it.

"She's letting us borrow a shovel?"

"Looks like it."

"Why would she do something like that?"

Sam shrugged offhandedly.

"Hey, is she an old girlfriend or something? You're acting kind of weird."

Sam opened the door, picked up the shovel and examined the blade with great care. "The two of us thought we might go out to dinner tonight, if you didn't mind."

Hunter backhanded his mouth, smiling as if he'd discovered some forbidden knowledge. "She is, isn't she?"

"Let's go clamming, Hunter." Sam weighed the shovel handle in his hands. "I'd like to show you how."

"You're changing the subject."

"You need to understand what it means when someone doesn't answer your questions. It means that person doesn't want to start a discussion."

With shovel in hand and the tide waning, they stepped over rocks of bloodstone and pyrite, agates and shale. Sam showed Hunter how to find the most promising spots for clams. The boy dug, piercing the earth, digging deep and fast into the watery sand while his uncle gave directions.

The clams burrowed with astonishing speed. After about a dozen fruitless tries, Hunter finally quit, spearing the ground with the shovel and leaving it to stand. "No wonder she gave you this stupid thing. It's no use. There's no clams on this beach."

"That's what everybody says when they start." For days now, Sam had been afraid to touch his nephew. He'd needed to, he knew that, but the gesture had felt contrived. Now, with great care, he cupped his hand against Hunter's neck, gave the boy's head a fond jostle. This time, it felt right. "That's what *I* said, too. But they're down there, Hunter. It's patience and timing. You're coming along."

Walking back, they stopped to examine tide pools that had appeared in bowls of rock. They found a green sea anemone lying open like a flower, boldly colored sea slugs, tiny undersea sponges. They watched a thumbnail-sized hermit crab scurry along in a borrowed shell.

A flock of seagulls scuttled behind them, curious and

fat, the wet sand mirroring their white bellies and gray wings. Something caught Sam's eye in the distance and, when he surveyed the heavy smudge of blue that marked the meeting of sea and sky, he saw a plume of water.

"There's a pod of whales out there," he told Hunter, placing his hand on the boy's shoulder again. "Most migrate north and south along the coast, but there's a group of grays that spends the year here. Can you see?"

Hunter shaded his eyes, shook his head. "No."

"There to your left. Look where I'm pointing, as far out as the eye can see."

"I don't—"

"There goes another plume. It's a whale, Hunter. It's spouting."

Hunter stepped away from Sam's touch. "You know so much about this place." He picked up a piece of beached kelp, the leaves dark and leathery, flung it high overhead. "When you came before, how much time did you spend here?"

"A week, maybe two weeks, each summer. With Mom and Dad."

"Why did you stop coming?"

As Sam spoke, he examined the horizon, couldn't find the whales anymore. The sun, which had hung overhead, had slipped almost imperceptibly toward the west. What had been a clear panorama now flashed and moved, impossible to see.

It occurred to Sam that Hunter was the same age now as he had been when he'd been running around these beaches with Aubrey. How could he have ever been so young?

"I grew up, I guess," he answered Hunter.

"That shouldn't make any difference."

"Or maybe I grew up because I had to stop coming, I don't know."

When he and Aubrey went out that night, Sam drove west, past the agate shop and the Old Cannery Building, rusted and foreboding, with the huge picture of a salmon on the side. They said nothing important to each other in the car. All was still and serene, two adults having a benign conversation together, until he mentioned that the car wasn't clean enough for her, and apologized because it smelled of dog. "I tried to clean it out when I found out I'd be driving you around. I took it to a car wash this morning, if that counts." He fumbled to roll down the window, and the car swerved a little bit.

"Careful." Aubrey grabbed her handle, and they laughed self-consciously at this being together, just the same as when they'd been teenagers. She was embarrassed that she had immediately chastised him, sounding like the wife or the mother she was.

"No sense getting in a car accident before we even get a chance to catch up."

"I had a car with automatic locks and windows," he explained as she cranked her own window down a bit, "but Ginny kept stepping on the knob and locking herself inside."

She had no right to the jealous urge that rose within her. She had never been able to picture Sam with someone else. A girl's name—

He glanced sideways at her as if he'd felt her go still. "Ginny. My golden retriever. Maybe we should have brought her with us, but she was lying on the carpet in there with her four paws up in the air. She has a bedtime she doesn't like to ignore."

"Oh." *Oh.* Aubrey shot him a smile.

This time he reached to pull out the ashtray and the car wobbled again.

She reached for the wheel to stabilize it. "What are you doing *now?* Let me do it. You're driving."

"You're sure?" he asked.

"Yes."

And he smiled. "My gum."

"What?"

"I was going to throw it away in the ash tray. I hate pitching gum out the window. Comes from too many years of finding it on the bottom of my shoe, I guess."

Aubrey held out her hand.

"You want it?"

"I'll wrap it in paper or something. I'd rather do it than die on the road." She couldn't keep the unbidden thought of the two of them being found dead on the road together from surfacing. What would her family think?

He placed the knot of gum in her hand, still warm and soft from his mouth, his front teeth marks like two dashes imprinted in it. She stared at the gum in her

179

hand for a moment too long, feeling years younger, a lovely curl in her stomach that she hadn't felt since she'd been a girl. One-handed, she fumbled in her purse and found a tissue. She tore this in half and folded his gum inside it, making a smaller and smaller square. She dropped the tissue inside his ashtray and shut it. For the longest time, as the fence posts blipped past like frames in a film, she stared out, not moving. When, with sharp little jerks, she started to crank the window up again, Sam said, "No, don't," reaching across to touch her arm. "Leave it open, too. It's nice."

The churning air changed the atmosphere in the car. For Sam, Covenant Heights and feeding the homeless and the parking-lot lighting and Joe dying and the disapproval of Grant Ransom all fell away. For Aubrey, the uncertainty of not knowing how to respond to her husband and the wet touch of her son's lips and the police calls in the night and Channing's slipping grades dissipated into nothing. Responsibility fell away; the hour belonged to them. They felt as young as two teenagers when the air rushed across and danced through their hair.

Sam straightened up, cocked his shoulder to one side, started driving with one hand, and curled his fingers possessively around the knob of the gearshift. Aubrey swept one hand through her hair and momentarily wished for a scarf, then thought, *Oh, I'll just let my hair blow in the wind, oh yes! I will!*

He turned the radio on and scanned the stations, ". . . controversy over the double play in the fifth inning . . . admission is free! You can't afford to miss it . . . for the Oregon News Network, I'm . . . really wins and loses when urban neighborhoods . . ." The scan finally stopped on music, light jazz with muted trumpets.

"I can't find anything good. What's good on the radio here?" he asked.

"I don't know. How should I know? I don't live here anymore."

"Well, you *used* to live here."

"There was K-Gull. KGUL. That's the only thing I remember."

He laughed.

"I know. It was cheesy, wasn't it?"

"What sort of music do you like?"

She hesitated, realizing she was treading dangerous waters, but couldn't stop herself. "The old stuff. The stuff we used to listen to." He started to punch buttons again. He found one oldies station playing "Our Day Will Come" by The Shirelles.

"This place *always* was a little cheesy," she said.

"No, it wasn't," he said. "It was wonderful."

"Is that why you brought your nephew here?" she asked. "Because it used to be wonderful?"

She saw him stiffen behind the wheel and avoid the question. "The kid's had a tough time."

She waited.

"His father just died."

"Your—" More pictures of his past came to mind—details she'd missed, dynamics she'd never known about and wished she had. He hadn't had any brothers that she knew of.

"My brother-in-law," he explained. "Brenda's husband."

"Oh." And she couldn't help but smile. "That's a strange thought. Little Brenda all grown up and married."

"Brenda hasn't been little for a long time."

"When are you going to tell me about yourself?" she asked him. "I can't imagine what your life must be like."

A coffee shop suddenly loomed. Ruby's, a neon coffee cup dripping drops of light from it that reflected in the gleam of the fresh blacktop. A sign beside the door said YES, WE ARE OPEN.

Sam signaled to turn in. "This look okay?"

She scooted forward in her seat. Her voice sounded disappointed even to her. "Let's go to the water first, Sam. I know this is supposed to be supper, but I don't think I could eat anything; I'm too excited to see you. Maybe later."

He let out a little laugh. "Well, some things about you have changed. Remember when you made me drive twenty-three miles to that place called Gladys Burger? Because of that fry sauce you liked?"

But when she answered, she wasn't smiling. She suddenly felt all of her age again, staring at the ringless fingers on her lap. Of course, this was for old-time's sake, nothing dangerous about it, she thought, as she fought the urge to hide her naked ring finger.

"Yes, Sam. Many things have changed."

A sign noting BEACH ACCESS appeared in the headlights. "Oh, there it is." He almost missed it, had to jerk the car without signaling to make the turn. They couldn't see the ocean with their eyes because of the darkness; they could only see it the way Sam had learned to help people see their way to faith—from the lights reflecting off the jetty, sensing the dark, liquid movement before them, the tossing of water being flung to the shore, the smell of salt and seaweed and crab.

Sam found a parking lot behind the Best Western motel and steered into an empty space. He cut the engine. The water seemed to roar at them through the open windows. For one beat too long, they sat without talking. "The windows," she said. "Should we roll them up so we can lock the car?"

"Guess so. Of course we should."

While he finished with his window and locked everything, she climbed out, stood at the side of the car hugging her shoulders as if she needed to hold herself back from something. He came around the fender, and stood.

A clapboard bridge led from the motel parking lot over clumps of high grass. In the distance, the moon illuminated pathway and sea. The appeal of the bridge's silhouette against the sea made her start toward it. She kicked off her shoes in the grass, while he bent over wingtip leather shoes, so different than anything Gary would wear. They left their shoes side by side in a shadowy pile. *We'll never find these again if we leave them here,* she thought, but it didn't seem important. Only staying beside him seemed important. When they walked barefooted on the sand together and felt the cool on their feet, it was as if they stepped into a distant past, a memory road they hadn't known they could travel again.

A long glass restaurant stretched the length of the pier, and as they came closer to it they could see a waitress moving from table to table. And then he started laughing, smiling up to the sky. "We were on the water at our cottages. We could have done this there, without driving so far."

"I know. But—"

"—but Hunter was there."

"Yes."

She gathered up the sides of her skirt in her hands. She turned out, to the sea. Drew close enough that, when the water tossed itself up over the sand, it rolled over her feet, too.

She shrieked. The chill of the water surprised her. No matter how often she returned, which had been any number of times, she never remembered the cold of the ocean. It took her breath away.

Oh, to wade farther into the ocean, not to look back, not to be sensible anymore! Oh, to pretend she was who she'd once been instead of being who she'd become! Instead, she made her way under the pier and down the beach.

"Hey, wait for me," Sam called, walking faster. Even before he caught up with her, his mind already toyed with the question. *Where did the both of you go, Aubrey? Where had your father taken you when I came that summer?*

Sam was breathless by the time she broke her stride. "How is your dad, Aubrey? What's going on with him?"

She stopped completely, her shoulders square to the shore. "My dad. You want to know about him? He lives on a boat not far from here, cut off from the world. Doesn't even have a telephone."

"Does he take people fishing anymore?"

"No."

Aubrey offered no more explanation than that. The word, her *no,* felt like a closed door. For the first time, Sam realized he'd always wondered if Walt McCart had done something to keep them apart from each other.

It wouldn't do, asking something like that now. Sam chastised himself for the habit he was falling into with her, charting out his every word. "All those years we spent looking across the water when we were children," he finally said. "Did you ever stop to wonder what's out there, no matter how far away it is, farther than we can see?"

She shrugged.

"Japan? The Midway Islands? But the Midway Islands are too far south, I think."

"There isn't much for a long way."

"Russia. Russia's out there. Is it even Russia anymore? There's all those new countries."

"All the world is out there, Sam. You just have to go

out there and come around the same way and there it is again."

"We used to look out all the time and think about it. Do you remember?"

"I do."

Then from somewhere along the point, a long distance off, someone began shooting fireworks over the water. The reflection was beautiful. Their lights sprang into the air and onto the water like flowers—each a bright color, red and flickering silver, a gold and a green—the sprinkles of light flying far before they began to flicker and sink to the ground.

Aubrey gave a little bleat of surprise when something black and heaving moved toward her legs in the water. It was a Boogie board, heavy and waterlogged. Sam laughed and held it toward the sky, teasing, "A gift! Thank you, Lord!"

"I guess it pays to hang out with a minister."

"Somebody must have lost it."

"It's soaked, though. It won't float."

"Maybe it will. You could try."

"Yeah, or *you* could."

"I'll get wet."

When she spoke, she included both of them in the dare. "But you *know* we'd both dry."

He held her arm as if he were trying to see her face in the dark. "I will if you will." It seemed, suddenly, that they might be talking about more than a swim.

She didn't give her answer right away. She was counting the cost, perhaps a meal in damp clothes, a soggy, shivering ride in the car.

"Something else about you that has changed. You never used to think twice about things when you were young."

"Shut up," she said, batting at him. "You said I hadn't changed. You lied, then."

How dare he think she was afraid? He hadn't gone in yet either. She began running toward the waves, laughing, flinging her arms into the sky, and the water crested a little. Suddenly it came, crashing into her, almost knocking her down. Before she knew what had happened, Sam was there beside her. He had the board, was trying to ride it, but it went under and so did he.

"Sam!" she called, laughing. "You're crazy."

He surfaced, sputtering, his hair flat against his head until it shook it out like a dog.

"Come in," he said. "Come all the way in."

She had no choice. Another breaker broadsided her and she dove beneath it. For seconds, she didn't know which direction was up or down. The water boiled around her. She didn't know whether it tugged her deeper or buoyed her toward the surface. When her head emerged, she and Sam were together, waves alternately lifting them and letting them fall.

Aubrey had never seen stars so bright as the ones above them. They swam in a heavenly sea of their own. She splashed Sam. He retaliated by taking two strokes and dunking her.

They didn't stay in long. The water was much too cold for that. Their clothes were plastered against their bodies when they traipsed out. When they dried, their skin would be filmed with salt. Sam left the sodden Boogie board on the shore for someone else to find. "Come here," he said, watching her shiver. He'd brought a blanket for himself, but he drew close and wrapped it around her shoulders instead. "You're freezing."

"S-so are, are you."

He held the blanket tight at the hollow of her throat, and Aubrey stood with fists together inside of it, clenching it shut. *We could share the blanket,* she thought to say. But she didn't want to share. She didn't want to stand that close to him, to be wrapped together inside something warm. When they started walking back, she felt the light pressure of Sam's guiding hand in the small of her back, felt his fingers slide possessively to the base of her spine. His chivalry sent an unwanted current through her. *How many years had it been since Gary had been chivalrous? How many years since he had held a door open for her or taken her hand or guided her along like a man protecting his wife?*

A group of teenage girls was heading toward them, bare feet plodding along the sand. One of them, who remarkably reminded her of Channing, carried a flashlight. The girls giggled and screamed as the flashlight's beam arced back and forth across the ground. One of the girls cried, "There's a crab. Don't step on the crab."

"Be careful," Sam whispered conspiratorially to Aubrey. "It's dark out here and there's a crab in the sand and we're barefooted."

"We keep telling each other to be careful. Have we both changed that much?" Aubrey asked as they walked, their steps cradled in cool, soft sand.

"I was the careful one," he said, reminding her. "But you, you never were."

CHAPTER SEVENTEEN

Finding their shoes proved to be a chore. Neither had realized, as they'd hurried toward the water, that each access looked somewhat the same, each marked by a small walkway, low shrubbery, a wooden bridge with rails over the dunes. Even with the sand lit by the moon, it was almost impossible to stumble across where they had been.

"This is fine with me," Aubrey kept babbling along, talking mostly to keep her teeth from chattering. "I can do without those shoes. I have another pair."

But Sam kept searching through empty clumps of grass. "They won't let us into a restaurant—"

"We're wet from head to foot. Shoes are the least of our worries. We'll stop at one of the tourist shops, buy a cheap pair of flip-flops." Then, looking at him, she realized, "You don't want to leave your shoes behind, do you? Those were your best shoes. You wore your best shoes to the beach."

He didn't say a word.

"Those were Sunday shoes. You probably *preach* in those shoes."

"Well," he said almost apologetically, "I do."

"You can't afford to lose your shoes, huh?"

"It would set me back a week's pay."

She gave an exaggerated sigh. "Things were so much easier before we grew up."

He wouldn't let them leave until they searched more. When they finally found the right bridge, the right steps, the right low shrubbery, Aubrey slid into her sandals without ado. He sat on the steps to put on his socks, brushing sand off the soles of his feet. As he tied his shoes and she watched him leaning over his work, she stared at the crown of his head, the hair that whorled around his cowlick in the shape of a galaxy. Oh, how she'd always loved the color of his hair!

If I could go back, would I want to? If we could turn back the clock . . . ?

Her throat caught and nothing seemed quite so innocent anymore.

"You ready?" He looked up at her as he made one final tug on his shoe strings.

"Maybe we should just go back to the cottages," she suggested, "not eat anything tonight."

"I'm starving, Aubrey."

"Don't you think we ought to change clothes or something?"

"Well, I wouldn't mind, but I'd have to explain it to—"

"—your nephew."

"Yes."

"He'd want to know why we went swimming in our clothes."

"He'd ask lots of questions."

They were both thinking the same thing as Sam stood and did his best to brush off his slacks. Neither of them was ready to share this momentous renewal of friendship, its joy, its awkwardness. *It would never do for Hunter to read something into this that he ought not to.* It was too new to them, the monumental exchanging of history, the giving credence to their past.

They returned to Ruby's coffee shop on foot, deciding that walking might be the best way to dry their clothes. They slid into a booth and the waitress handed them menus while Aubrey unconsciously tucked a strand of hair behind her ear. It annoyed her that Sam had dried with relative grace. He sat across from her now, perusing the descriptions of hamburgers and sandwiches, his shirt looking crisp even though it had been in the ocean. His face was more handsome than it had ever been, his hair falling in endearing wisps against his temples.

Sam glanced up from his menu and said, as if he'd read her mind, "You look good. You know that?" He measured her with his eyes.

"I don't. I've been swimming." And the years had changed her. She tried to read the menu, but couldn't.

"You're wrong about that. The ocean did wonders for you."

In spite of the late hour, Ruby's was busy. Music blared from the jukebox, much too loud. They inclined toward each other so they'd be able to hear. "Now I know what you mean. I look better when I've been dunked."

"Well," he said, grinning. "Somebody had to do it."

The waitress came to take their order, she a bowl of seafood chowder and he a burger cooked medium-well with cheddar cheese and bacon. (You don't want something like a Gladys burger? he'd insisted. You don't want something with fry sauce? No, she'd reassured him. I'm fine with soup.)

As quickly as that, the playfulness between them dwindled, replaced by silence. "What do you think about this?" Sam asked at last. "What do you think the Lord is doing, bringing us together again like this?"

She remembered Sam mentioning his faith when he'd been young; she had taken it in stride then, accepted it because it was a part of him. But now she felt too raw from battling her husband's disease, would tell Sam that she could never accept that any of this might be *planned* by something. She remembered discussing it with Sam once on the beach. *I don't believe in God. I believe in the sea.*

"Tell me about you, Aubrey. Tell me about your life, what you've been doing since I last saw you."

My husband is in an institution, she might have said, *there's been a struggle in our lives for a long time. The children think we're on a trip together because I didn't want their worlds to be shaken.*

Aubrey realized she'd much rather be on the beach with Sam, diving into the breakers, hidden by darkness and the pounding of the surf on the sand, than face-to-face in the harsh light of a coffee shop, trying to explain her life. Sam was so familiar to her, yet he'd become a stranger, too. She had no way to know who he'd become, or how she ought to see him.

"I'm married," Aubrey told him simply, her hands folded in front of her chin. "I have three kids. I have pictures of them in my purse."

She glanced around the booth for her purse before she remembered she'd left it locked in the car.

"They're all beautiful. I can't wait for you to see."

"How old are they?"

"Like stairsteps. Hannah is four. She's the baby. Channing is the oldest. She's fifteen, going on twenty."

"A four-year-old *and* a teenager?"

"And there's Billy in the middle. He's eight. His ultimate goal is to be a soccer player and to make it to old age having worn only one pair of underwear. *Spiderman* underwear."

"A typical male."

"You got it." Aubrey had thought she'd never stop shivering. But Sam's proximity, his body angled toward hers, his wrist aligned next to her elbow, warmed her. "How about you? I want to hear about *your* family."

"Your husband's name," Sam said, as she realized he wasn't going to be easily diverted. "What is it?"

"Gary." She couldn't explain why she hesitated. "Gary Mangelson."

"So you're—?"

"Aubrey Mangelson."

"It's hard to think of you with a different name." She

saw emotion working Sam's face, as if it cost him something to process the thought. "How did you meet him? How did you meet this Mr. Gary Mangelson?"

"At work. Someone introduced us at a Christmas party, he asked me out, and we married a year later. It's a pretty predicable story."

Sam examined the tines of his fork.

"It was a marine manufacturing company. A company that made upholstery for boats. In Portland. That's where we both worked."

"And now?"

"I may look for something after Hannah starts school full-time. Gary stayed, moved up through the ranks into management. We've done okay on one income."

"You're happy?" he asked, watching her face.

"I am," she lied.

The waitress arrived, carrying their plates. She set a towering burger in front of Sam, a bowl of soup in front of Aubrey. Aubrey unwrapped her silverware and placed the flimsy napkin in her lap. She watched Sam rearrange his pickles and lift his tomato to see what might be underneath. They were both biding their time until the waitress left them alone again.

"It's your turn," she insisted as he reached for the mustard bottle. "I asked you questions first, but you've done nothing but interrogate me."

Sam ticked subjects off on his fingers. "No kids. Never been married."

She nodded.

"I went to seminary after college and started

preaching in a little church with two dozen members. The church I'm in now is much larger."

"That's good, isn't it?"

"I spend time with my dad once a week. My mother has Alzheimer's but we're dealing with that."

"You compartmentalize everything."

"Doesn't everyone when they're having a conversation like this one? Brenda married a man named Joe. He became a close friend, like the brother I never had."

"He's Hunter's father. The one who died."

Sam fingered his water glass, wiping away moisture. "Yes."

"How sad for Brenda."

"I keep thinking about that. Maybe I haven't given her the support I could have."

"You have Hunter."

"That took a bit of doing."

Aubrey found herself gauging him, debating whether or not she ought to ask this next question. She couldn't turn away from it.

"You're in a Protestant church, aren't you? Does your position keep you from marrying?"

He set his half-eaten hamburger on his plate and squared his shoulders. "I'm allowed to marry. There's just never been—"

He trailed off, unwittingly leaving it open to her imagination.

"Hasn't there been someone, Sam? Someone you've wanted to spend your life with?"

"It's tricky," he said. "I counseled a woman once who

I considered dating. But God had other plans for her. She'd gotten divorced and the Father put her marriage back together again."

A jumble of emotions played through her, sorrow that he'd been alone all this time, relief because it meant he was unchanged.

"That's an amazing story for her. Miraculous."

"I've seen a lot of miracles," he noted glibly.

"But maybe not in your own life," she said, pointing at him with her soup spoon, pinning him down.

"It's tricky. I said that, didn't I? Everyone at Covenant Heights is watching."

"I can see how it would be difficult."

"There's usually a painful choice to be made. Whatever I do affects other people."

"That's the name of your church? Covenant Heights?"

"Yes. And your husband's name is Gary."

"Yes."

"Look at both of us," he said. "We were so young, then, do you remember?"

"Oh, yes. I remember."

"I thought I'd always spend my life with you."

CHAPTER EIGHTEEN

Aubrey lay in bed that night, her eyes dry from lack of sleep, her heart aching for what might have been. Sam's words ran through her mind like a dangerous spring.

I thought I'd always spend my life with you.

Her throat went coarse with emotion when the cell phone rang. Aubrey's heart skipped a beat. Oh, how she wished this would be Gary! Oh, how she needed to hear her husband's voice on the line. She needed Gary not as he'd become, but different, strong and healthy, wrapping his words around her, strengthening her.

Even as she flipped open the phone and tried to read the number, Aubrey knew she wouldn't hear the voice she longed for. That voice didn't exist. And the treatment center wouldn't allow Gary to call for 72 hours anyway, not until he made it through detox.

"Mommy?"

The moment Aubrey heard the little voice, she came fully awake. "Hannah?" The number she'd read through bleary eyes began to register. Channing's cell phone. Which meant her two girls were together at Emily's, taking care of each other.

"I just can't sleep without Elephant."

Aubrey squeezed her eyes shut, relief and distress filling her in equal measure. "Of course you can't."

"Channing said I could call you on her phone."

"I'm glad she did. "

"Were you asleep, Mommy?"

"No," Aubrey said. "I was awake, too."

"Is Daddy asleep? Can I talk to him?"

"Oh, Sweetie." She hated herself for the tears that began to come. "He isn't—" Aubrey stopped herself, remembering the story she and Gary had decided to tell the children. *One falsehood leads to so many others.* "He isn't awake."

"I miss you. I want to be with you and Daddy."

"I know." With sharp, purposeful movements, Aubrey swiped at her tears. "We miss you, too."

"Aunt Emily made us eat Brussels sprouts."

"I'm sorry about that."

"I put them in my pocket."

"Oh, honey."

"Mommy, I *had* to."

So difficult, trying to sound stern when she wanted to laugh and cry at the same time. "I'll tell you what. In the morning when Aunt Emily wakes up, I'll talk to her and get her to help you pick out a new animal at the store."

"No, that isn't it. I don't want a *different* animal. I only want Elephant."

"You'll have to make do, Hannah." *We're all having to make do with what we've been given.* "I'm sorry we couldn't turn around, but you three might have missed the plane."

Such a plaintive little voice, it tore at Aubrey's heart. "I like the way Elephant *smells.* I like him because he's *blue.* I like him because he doesn't have fur on his ear and he only has one eye."

Is this the way life is? Aubrey thought. *Do we look for something that isn't right to replace something we had to leave behind?*

"Hannah, Sweetie. Don't cry. I can hear you crying."

"I c-can't help it."

"Get Channing to give you a big hug for me, okay? Get her to rub your back until you can fall asleep."

I have to protect them from Gary's failure, don't I? If I don't, they'll lose respect for him the same way that I have.

Hannah's sniffing was pitiful. "O-okay."

"That's a girl."

"Mommy, when can we come *home?*"

Aubrey clutched the cell with both hands, longing for something that didn't exist anymore.

Oh, Gary, It's your fault. You're the one who has broken trust with your family.

"I don't know, Sweetie," she whispered. But she was thinking: *Our home may never be the same again.*

The seal pup arrived on the beach the same day that Hunter began to make friends.

Several hundred yards north of the cottages, a rock escarpment rose from the beach. Powerful breakers had swept it, bashing into it, exploding and flying skyward in a thousand sun-laced drops. Over the years, the falling droplets had carved a broad shell. Above this stood a headland where the soil had washed away, revealing roots knotted like seaman's ropes. It was in this quiet hollow, this shaded place, where the harbor seal appeared in late afternoon.

Sam had seen the posted signs even when he'd been a boy, hand scribbled by naturalists or printed off by the motels along Highway 1. SEAL PUPS REST ON SHORE. DO NOT DISTURB THEM! IT'S THE LAW! Or: HARBOR SEALS BRING THEIR YOUNG TO SHORE WHEN THEY TIRE OR WHEN SURF IS ROUGH. REMEMBER: SHARE

Sam had longed to stumble upon one of these infant seals when he'd been young. Although he'd vowed never to touch or harm one, Sam had ached for the experience of standing close, just once to examine the placement of whiskers on such a small, wild thing, to read indelible life shining from its round eyes. But he had never been lucky enough for it, or maybe he had just never been chosen.

Seal pups had been as elusive to him as Aubrey's magical green phosphorescence that she bragged she often saw flash in the waves at sundown.

The Pontiac had pulled into the cottage parking space shortly after noon, its grill and its California license plate splattered with bugs from a journey. Sam watched the parents, two boys about Hunter's age, and a teenage girl with bobbed hair stumble out and stretch and exclaim over the sea. He'd been standing there thinking of Aubrey. *What was she doing? Had she talked to her kids, her husband? Was she trying to stay away from him after what he'd said last night?* Glad for the diversion, Sam stepped across the lawn.

He thrust his hand forward in greeting, and exchanged pleasantries. "I'm next door." "How long you staying?" And to the kids, "I've got a nephew about the same age as you. Don't know where he's gone off to."

If the teens had been the least bit shy, Hunter never would have been invited into the pack. But Sam watched as the careful dance began, adolescents moving in circles around each other, the girl catching Hunter's eye, one of the boys waving and shouting, "You had any luck fishing off the pier?"

By three, with the sun growing low enough to cast spiked shadows along the hummocks of grass, the four were chattering like they'd known each other for years and renovating a fire pit on the leeward side of the dunes. Yesterday the spot had been barely visible, full of sand and half-charred trash, rocks coated with soot and shattered from someone else's bonfire. Today Hunter and his friends carted away the broken stones and carried in new ones. They dug a deep hole, making good use of Aubrey's shovel. They dragged up lengths of driftwood, worn as smooth as bone by the surf.

He could not have said when Hunter disappeared down the beach. One of the boys knocked on Sam's door and asked, "Hey, is Hunter hanging out here? My brother can't find him." And Sam shrugged. "I don't know."

"We didn't want to start the fire without him."

"Maybe I'll have a walk up the beach," Sam volunteered, grateful for a chance to release his pent-up energy. "If I find him, I'll tell him you're looking for him."

He set out in search of his nephew, leaving Ginny behind, unable to walk past Aubrey's cottage without glancing in its direction. *What was keeping her away from him?* Her lights hadn't been turned on all day; the curtains were open, her car gone. *Aubrey was alone in this place, with no one to notice if anything went wrong, no one to notice if she didn't turn up.*

He ought to be the one taking care of her!

Sam was spared this self-indulgence when he caught sight of his nephew. Sam walked faster at first, hurrying to catch up with the boy, but he slowed when he saw Hunter's stance. The boy wasn't moving, his silhouette still, reflecting perfect lines in the mirror of wet sand. He gripped the shovel in one hand. The other hand did not clench or stir at his side.

The pup, dark and sleek, did not lift its head or struggle onto its flippers. It remained in the hollow where its mother had left it, staring at Hunter with curiosity, too young to be afraid.

Hunter did not even blink. Pieces of his sun-bleached hair lifted in the breeze, fell into place again. The boy must have gone motionless mid-stride, his limbs bent in the act of moving forward, a cat ready to spring.

The moment seemed to stretch into eternity, yet it couldn't have lasted a minute, a minute-and-a-half, at most. Sam couldn't breathe, measuring the expression of trust on the pup's face with Hunter's choice not to disturb it. The low sun became diamonds flung across open water. The seal pup adjusted its weight with its winged foot, leaving the imprint of a watery M.

From one slight change in Hunter's jaw, Sam could tell his nephew was smiling. Sam backed away, affording his nephew as much distance as the boy afforded the animal. This one moment represented everything he'd brought his nephew to the coast to see.

To break in and whisper, *Look, Hunter. Didn't I tell*

you it would be this way? didn't seem suitable.

To share it seemed almost to steal it. Best for Hunter not to know he had been there.

Sunset and fire. Drifting patterns of light being born, and of light being swept away. As the flames took hold of the kindling at their feet, the blaze drew its color from the sky. Brilliant yellows and crimsons burned above the sea.

When Sam returned, the kids were playing Frisbee in the waning light. He released Ginny and, bursting to freedom, she hurled herself after the plastic disc, too. A good number of cottage guests had drawn lawn chairs into a circle. Others had found perches atop driftwood. Sam joined them.

The open, dark windows of Aubrey's cottage stared at him like empty eyes.

You are mighty, and firm in your purpose.

Father, why have you reunited me with Aubrey now, when it's too late?

Someone brought out a package of wieners to roast over the bonfire. Eventually, as Sam was thinking about getting his guitar, Hunter returned. The California girl tugged at Hunter's arm, "Where did you go? We looked for you," and Hunter mumbled something cryptic while he let himself be coaxed into the fold. The boys welcomed him back with a good-natured shoving of shoulders.

Not until headlights slashed the darkness in the parking lot did Sam realize how concerned he'd become. His shoulders sagged in relief when Aubrey's lamp turned on. His chest tightened when he saw her drawing the curtains.

He who walks in wisdom is kept safe.

Sam made himself wait, knowing he hadn't any right to care what she'd been doing all day, knowing he had no right to this longing that blindsided him. He detached himself from the others when he saw her step off the patio into the sand. Later he would not remember how he'd come to stand beside her.

They spoke at the same time. "I had quite a day," she said.

"Whatever could have taken you so long?" he said.

"I didn't know you were waiting for me."

"I wasn't." An awkward pause. "But there's no one here to watch out for you.

"I talked to the kids. I went antiquing. There's a shop on Sailor Avenue with antique marbles. I walked the length of town. You didn't need for anyone to watch out for me."

"That's what I've been telling myself all day."

The fire cast moving flickers of light on her face and, for the first time, he saw her eyes were red and swollen from crying. "Aubrey, what is it? What's wrong?"

"It's nothing, Sam."

"I don't believe you."

"Just let me be."

She pulled free of his grasp and strode toward the others. By the time he'd caught up with her, someone had handed her a bag of marshmallows and she'd poked one onto a stick. Sam had a vague notion of her arm extending the branch over heat, the marshmallow pivoting, pivoting like the hands on a clock, as if it might still be measuring the days they'd had, the years they hadn't.

"I've never seen anyone so careful about roasting a marshmallow."

"I saw my father today," she said, focusing on the fire. "After all these years, you'd think he'd let down his guard with me. You'd think he'd stop shutting me out."

"Aubrey—"

"I expected him to at least ask questions about my family. There were things I wasn't certain about sharing with him. But he didn't even want to *know*."

"I'm sorry."

"You don't have to be sorry. I'm the one who decided to see him."

I've been watching him hurt you since you were twelve years old. All those years when he let you be the shadow and Kenneth be the star.

The marshmallow burst into flame. Aubrey made no attempt to rescue it.

"If I'd have gone with you," Sam said, "you wouldn't have had to drive home alone."

"You speak of being alone as if it's something to be frightened of."

"Blow the marshmallow out, would you? You're going to torch the whole place."

She swung it around, close enough to singe his eyebrows, and blew it out herself. When she pulled it off the stick and placed it in his mouth, Aubrey touched his lips.

Sam tried to swallow, and almost couldn't. He might as well be forcing down a lump of clay.

"Do you remember when I first kissed you?" *He shouldn't have asked. He knew better.*

"I'll never forget," she said.

Waves crashed onto shore in the darkness beyond them. The sound, usually comforting, turned to white noise in his head. An occasional burst of the teens' laughter twined into the air with the smoke.

The memory of that long-ago kiss hung between them.

Aubrey stood abruptly. "I brought pictures of the kids. You want to see them?" She fished in her pocket for a plastic sleeve that must have come from her bill-fold. She held the pictures out as if they were talismans that would protect them both. "This is Channing's school picture from last year. She's prettier than this, actually. She won't give a full smile because of her braces. This is the baby. Hannah. She won't take a picture without Elephant." The child was clutching a ragged, blue stuffed animal coming apart at the seams. "And this is Billy. He's such a precious little man. He was the only one who kissed me good-bye at the airport. Look at him, his face is always dirty. He always smells a little bit like sweat."

Sam almost *couldn't* look. Their smiling faces, Billy's toothy grin, made him ache. "I'd like to meet them," he said. "I bet we'd be friends."

"I bet so, too. Especially Billy."

"Channing looks like you."

"You think so?"

"She reminds me of you, bounding along the jetty."

"She's spent plenty of hours running around this beach."

The snapshots made Sam feel deficient, like the Biblical servant who had buried his master's coins and had nothing to show for them. *Oh, Father. If Aubrey had answered the door that day, is this something we would have had?*

"Is Gary—?" But he stopped because he had no right to ask the question. *Is Gary a good husband to you, Aubrey?* He didn't dare let himself finish it: *Because I would have been.*

He asked instead, "Your children, you say they spend lots of time here? Surely your father doesn't push them away?"

"No, he enjoys my children. It's just me. It's always been me—" Aubrey's stricken expression told him everything he needed to know.

CHAPTER NINETEEN

Sam purchased a kite on the wharf, an orange trapezoid with a spiral tail that snapped when it launched into the wind, and Hunter spent hours sending it skyward along the beach. While Hunter unfurled twine and ran backward along the beach, Aubrey coached through cupped hands, "That's it! Pull back!" and Sam caught it as it made mad lunges toward the sand.

Aubrey drove them along the coast toward the Umpqua Lighthouse, shore pines enclosing them when the road twisted inland, following the signs to Siltcoos Dunes. Every time the highway meandered west toward the headlands, she exclaimed over the broad expanse of sea. Sam treated them to ice cream when they stopped to browse at the cheese factory, Tillamook Mudslide for Hunter, blueberry cheesecake for Aubrey, and a double dip of pistachio pecan for himself. Hunter bought wind chimes for his mother. And for the next forty miles, every time they passed a sign about Siuslaw National Park, Hunter begged to rent dune buggies.

Sam couldn't resist dune buggies any more than his nephew could. He rented them at a place called Sandman Adventures. After donning helmets and revving their engines, they followed a path through oat grass and cypress until it opened onto what seemed like a planet of sand.

Aubrey let out a war whoop and headed straight uphill. Hunter followed, the orange flag flapping on the rear of his buggy. Sam kept some distance back, taking it all in. He might be in a landscape penned by some moody artist who kept shifting his brush, altering heights, rearranging patterns and forms. Sam had the feeling, if he arrived at the same place tomorrow, he wouldn't be in the same place at all. This sand moved, caught, overtook everything. If he stayed still long enough, he might simply disappear.

"What's taking you so long, Sam Tibbits?" Aubrey whipped around a dune and came at him full bore. He floored the buggy and hung a U, leading her toward a crest of sand that had been purled by the wind. Hunter zipped past them both, his fist raised and his T-shirt billowing. The three of them caught air, racing full-throttle toward the bottom.

They headed home after their rides wearing sunburn lines shaped like their goggles and grins as wide as Depoe Bay. Their scalps were gritty with sand. They found an oldies station; Aubrey sang along with *Rock Lobster*, only hitting every second or third note. She broke off the song to tell Hunter, "We were on the beach once and your uncle thought he was catching a sea otter in his hands. He grabbed it and it was nothing but an old shoe. Did he tell you about that?"

"What about the time she knocked over the bucket and we had crabs scuttling under the seats in the boat. Make her tell you about that."

"I'll bet your uncle never told you about the Sea Basket on all-you-can-eat night and they made his parents leave because he ate 167 shrimp."

"Stop," Sam said, chuckling, knowing they could tell Hunter stories about their childhood until his eyes rolled back in his head. "You're tormenting my nephew."

"I'm tormenting *you*," she said, poking him and laughing, before she reverted to singing *Rock Lobster* again.

• • •

When Sam donned running shoes and took Ginny for a jog on the beach, he passed an old pier that had fallen into ruin. Thick-napped grass carpeted the pilings. Rivulets of water had receded with the tide, sculpturing the sand.

Sam hadn't noticed the old church before; he realized it had been years since he'd come this far afield. As he ran, his footfalls plowed into the sand, his calf muscles burning, his lungs ready to burst. Every footstep called her name. *Aubrey. Aubrey.*

The morning was cool, the church's steeple impaling the fog. Sam couldn't place this tall, hand-cut stone building among his boyhood memories, but he knew it had been here. The cemetery outside was marked with headstones that must be a century old.

When he commanded Ginny to stay and pulled open the door of the church, wonderful old smells greeted him: the remnants of gladioli and carnations, vanilla candle wax, furniture polish and silver cleaner. Underneath was another smell, musty and biting, part mildew and part sweat.

Father, the troubles of my heart are as deep as the ocean.

The stained glass depicted not Bible stories but pictures from the sea. A lighthouse on a jagged rock. A boat pitching at sea. The sun fell through the windows in strands that spotlighted the dust motes. The ceiling towered over him as Sam neared the altar.

You brought me into a spacious place. Yet all you've

done is heap questions on my head.

Sam didn't expect anyone to greet him this time of morning. He meant only to walk forward along the center aisle, where holes had been worn in the carpet so the backing could be seen poking through, where decades of couples must have stood to exchange vows, where coffins had been set and wept over, where followers had come to say they would be baptized, where broken souls had come to accept Christ, and healing had taken place.

Search me and know me, Lord, because I don't know myself.

A man stepped down from the balcony but Sam did not notice him at first. For some reason, Sam expected the minister here to wear robes and a stole even in the middle of the week. So he was surprised to see the man dressed in a pair of faded jeans and a scrubby green shirt, looking more like a grizzled fisherman than someone who served the church.

The minister said quietly, "Welcome," and went about slowly carrying a plate holding unleavened bread to the altar. Sam watched while the man's hands broke the bread into pieces. He headed out a side door and returned some minutes later with a chalice. He set it, too, on the altar.

"You're just in time for communion. The sanctuary is always open, but on Wednesdays we offer the elements of the Lord's Supper."

Sam focused on the stained glass overhead, a ship in a storm aiming toward a distant lighthouse. In the panes of the window, the beacon from the lighthouse had been cut from clear, faceted glass, reflecting diamonds. The shards of blue were transparent but filmy, a watercolor hazed with oil.

"Solomon Fraser." He extended his hand.

They shook hands soundly. "Sam Tibbits. Pastor Sam Tibbits."

"Ah, you're here on vacation?"

Sam didn't know how to answer. It hadn't been his choice to take a sabbatical. He wondered how this time might have been different if he had sought it out for himself.

He wondered if God would've been more inclined to point him the right direction if he had not been so certain he was already headed there.

Upon the altar, candle flames dipped and waltzed on a gentle draft. A telephone rang from some distant office, muted and urgent. The waiting communion cup and the plate of unleavened bread stood at the foot of the altar, as inviting as a banquet laid out for a hungry guest.

Sam didn't realize he hadn't answered until Solomon said, "If you feel capable of doing something, Sam Tibbits, then God isn't the one doing the calling."

When Sam first understood the Father wanted him to preach, he had not once, not ever, *ever,* questioned that what was happening to him had been divine inspiration. He had prayed ever since he'd been a boy, in the child-like way of a boy, that the Father would use his life for something special. Sam had only batted .243 his junior year in American Legion, so the professional baseball career was out of the question.

"God has done nothing since he brought me here except make me *remember*," he said to Solomon.

I'm desperate for you, Father. I'm desperate for your guidance.

Solomon lifted the plate of bread from the altar, gave thanks over it, and held it toward Sam. It occurred to Sam that he was standing in the precise spot where he'd stood earlier, where the carpet was worn flat by people who had stepped forward.

Solomon recited from the Bible, "This is my body given for you; do this in remembrance of me."

In remembrance of me.

Oh, Father.

Sam was standing where people had fallen on their knees in joy. He was standing where people had knelt in pain.

"This cup is the new covenant in my blood," Solomon recited. "Do this, whenever you drink it, in remembrance of me."

Come back to your first love, Beloved.

Sam dipped the bread inside the cup. He waited until the bread was soaked deeply with the ruby liquid. He put the bread on his tongue, holding it there, tasting both grapes and pungent wheat. It tasted like nothing Sam had ever tasted before. Yet it tasted as familiar and sweet as the first time he'd taken communion as a child.

Oh, thank you, Father.

"You must remember," Solomon said when Sam

opened the massive door to leave, "that you are not called to fix people. You are called to love them. And sometimes that is the more difficult job."

On Thursday morning, while mist still curtained the sky, Aubrey knocked on their cottage door to say she'd rented a crab boat. Not twenty minutes later, they were dressed and ready. Even Hunter was excited to be on the wharf so early in the day. Seagulls already swirled around boats in the bay. People shouted to one another in the slips. A bell clanged from a distant buoy.

As Sam watched Aubrey step onto the planks of the dock, now painted bright yellow when once they'd been weathered gray, the wave of nostalgia hit him so hard that it knocked his breath away. The tall posts, which once had held a weathered McCart sign, now bore a ruby-red metal sign with block words in white: WHALE WATCHING. BOATS TO LET.

On the opposite side of the dock from where they were standing, a metal building displayed pictures of gray whales in the window.

Long ago, that metal building hadn't been there, either. That was the shack where Arlie kept the schedule book with green quadrille paper; a binder with rusty rings and bent edges. Where Arlie would lean on the long counter that held candy bars and plastic-jelly lures in every color. Where the pictures of *The Westerly*, the *No Nonsense*, and the *Stately Mary* had been tacked on the wall.

If he looked hard enough, Sam could almost see Kenneth McCart swabbing down the decks, leaping with sure steps from the wharf with the coiled green hose in his hand.

The boat Aubrey had rented was a bare aluminum skiff, as dented as an offroader's hubcap. It rocked as Hunter stepped in. The proprietor loaded supplies for the trip, buckets, a bag of frozen bait, Styrofoam floats, and crab rings constructed of mesh, their rims bound thickly with black rubber.

Sam yanked the rope on the single outboard and, with a chuff of oily blue smoke, the motor came to life. The skiff rose and fell with the chop. Aubrey showed Hunter how to bait the crab rings, how to drop them, how to space them evenly. And Hunter discovered what the other two already knew as they made circles and checked the pots that day: The thrill wasn't only in luring crabs, but also in deciding which ones to keep.

The crabs had to be scrutinized, the widths of their shells measured from point to point. The crabs scurried about, their legs making amusing clicking noises along the bottom of the metal skiff. Breeding females had to be thrown back. Any crabs that measured a hair under $5\frac{3}{4}$ inches had to be tossed, too.

They ended up with precious few in the bucket!

It was just after noon when they hauled in their gear and counted their catch. Nine Dungeness crabs, enough for a reasonable supper. Sam headed the boat into the harbor, steering them around the spit, where the seal herd had hauled out onto the shore. The largest one sprawled in the driest, warmest spot, sunning its belly. Others crowded around him, their bodies strewn across the sandbar like wrinkled, fat sausages. Pups frolicked among the adults, capering about on their flippers.

Hunter started to rise but Sam placed a hand on his shoulder.

"Not while we're underway, buddy. Keep your seat."

Hunter craned his neck. "We can't get any closer?" His nephew didn't mention his encounter with the seal pup.

Sam throttled down the engine, edging toward shore. An easy surf slapped the skiff. The only other sounds were the sporadic barks of the seals, a ship's horn blowing, the jeers of seagulls circling overhead. The water evened out, began to quiet, became murky. Beneath the hull it flowed like smelted pewter, heavy and still.

Hunter stayed amidship, his rapper-logo cap pulled low to shade his face. Sam could tell the boy was disappointed when he cut the motor completely.

"We mustn't go closer. The ones out fishing, who need to feed their pups, might be afraid to return to shore."

"We'd be careful. Nobody would know about it."

"We mustn't take the chance of harming them."

Even as Sam said the words, he was struck by Aubrey's posture opposite him. Not knowing she was being watched, she huddled in the boat with her arms hugging her legs, her shoulders curled forward in defeat. She watched the seals absently while she bit her bottom lip. Sam sensed her sadness, almost stronger than her body could bear.

Are you missing your father's love, Aubrey? Or are you hiding something more?

Solomon Fraser's words echoed in his head. *Not called to fix people. Called to love them.*

Oh, Aubrey. I have loved you since I was eleven years old.

Hunter touched his arm. "Look." A seal and her pup had surfaced on their starboard side. Two gleaming heads, one small and one large, bobbed above the ripples. The sea mammals didn't seem afraid. Sam could see the pinpricks of their whiskers; he could almost touch them. Their eyes were as inquisitive as children.

As silently as the seals appeared, they slipped underwater and were gone.

Even Aubrey had lifted her chin to see them. Sam clapped his nephew's shoulder, this time in love and not restraint. "The Lord sometimes blesses with a physical sign, Hunter. Something he lets you see so you'll know he is nearby. Something that becomes dear to you."

"The seals?"

Sam's eyes leveled on the boy's. "Watch and see. I believe so."

CHAPTER TWENTY

Hunter steered the skiff alongside the pier while Aubrey brandished the bucket proudly, showing it off to the dockhand. "Not a bad catch for one morning, is it?"

Sam pitched the stern rope onto the wharf and jumped. After he attached the boat to its mooring, he offered Aubrey his hand. She shook her head, loving the feeling of the breeze in her hair. When their fingers interlaced, they fit together as if they'd been wrought for this one purpose. Sam's grip carried her back to a dozen other moments, to a handful of other sunswept summers, days when Sam had raced her along the jetty and they'd counted cranes roosting among the rocks and he'd kissed her. Sam's grip transported her to days when her future seemed full of possibility and she'd thought her father would forgive her and she hadn't been married to a man enslaved by drinking.

Gary can't hurt himself. He's taken care of. He can't hurt other people.

But what of the day he comes home?

Aubrey hoisted herself from the skiff. She had things she needed to tell Sam. She had questions to ask of him as well. *If you are the pastor of a church, how can you be here so long?* She wanted to know. But every time they were together, she felt so lighthearted. She knew how brittle words could shatter that façade. Aubrey asked instead, "Who's boiling and cleaning the crabs?" while she removed her hand from his. She could tell by the quick tilt of his head that he'd noticed. So difficult, pretending Sam's touch no longer had any effect on her.

"Oh, I thought we ought to let Hunter do that."

Aubrey had cleaned plenty of Dungeness in her day. Walt McCart had taught her to boil them in a monstrous pot and gut them almost before she'd been old enough to buckle her shoes. She could have dismembered a number of them and had them in a plastic bag in minutes. But today she had no stomach for the task. "Ah, you're sparing him no experience, Sam."

"I'm not. The boy has to learn."

The playful banter began again. "I remember when *you* learned."

"I believe *you* taught me."

"I believe I did."

Hunter ran along ahead of them, swinging the bucket. Salt hazed the air, heightening the sense of distance from one spot to another. From where they stood, their view was one of constant motion, surf foaming on the shore, boats bobbing at their moorings, dunegrass bowing to the wind. The sun shattered across the water.

As the boy's form receded, Aubrey said, "My father doesn't discuss my mother. He doesn't talk about her at all. Did you notice that?"

His shirt had gone limp in the damp breeze. He yanked at his buttons, centering them upon his chest. "We were kids. We had so many other things going."

"I barely remember my mother. I remember her flying a kite with Kenneth. She had a yellow bathing suit with polka dots."

"How old were you when she died?"

"Not old enough to remember what she looked like. Hannah's age, isn't that odd?"

"You told me. Hannah is—"

"—four. I was four."

"Surely you've seen pictures of your mother. Your

dad would have kept those."

"There are no pictures. He threw them out."

The pungence of fish, the dank aroma of mud and muck between the rocks, filled the air. Aubrey bent to pick up an oystershell, its underside rough enough to nick her hand. She cupped it inside her palm, its bowl as smooth as pearl.

"My whole life, I've watched my father ignore things that hurt."

"He needs to know it can't work that way. Ignoring things doesn't make them go away. It makes them get bigger."

The shell glinted, opalescent in her hand.

"Sometimes God heals us by letting us plow through something. That's what I think."

"I had forgotten what it was like to talk to you, Sam." Aubrey circled her thumb inside the shell. "I could always tell you anything. No one's ever listened to me like you do."

Hunter slogged toward a thick slab of rock some thirty feet away, his sneakered feet making small splashes in the surf. They were catching up with him. "You could take off your shoes, you know!" Sam shouted through cupped hands.

But Hunter was deafened by the wind. They watched him claim the rock, climbing atop it, lifting the bucket with his hands, a king claiming a territory. They watched him find a spot for the bucket before he explored a few mossy crevices, examining stones, pitching them underhand into the sea.

He stooped low to pull up a wet ribbon of kelp clustered with mussels. "These look good," he shouted to them. "Since we're cooking everything else, can we take these, too? Anybody got a knife?"

Aubrey pitched her own shell aside and fished a pocketknife from her purse. She rambled, "This ought to do. Be careful, it's sharp," while Sam rolled his pants past his calves. He was just yanking the final fold when, in a fit of bravery, she said, "I envy you, do you know that? I envy how you've always been so certain of things."

Sam straightened. She didn't understand why, but he sounded almost angry at her. "Certain of things?"

"Yes."

"You don't know what you're talking about."

"Sam?"

She hadn't meant to be reckless. But her words changed something between them.

She could tell by the square of his shoulders, the resolute way he marched out to Hunter, that her remark had opened a wound. She could tell by the jut of his elbow as he severed mussels from kelp. She could tell by the way he tromped back to shore with his nephew at his side, snapping the knife shut, setting it precisely in the middle of her palm.

"Sam?" she asked again. But Hunter kept beside them for the rest of the afternoon, swinging the bucket, babbling on about crabbing and viewing the harbor seals. She tagged along, confused and distracted, while Sam and Hunter borrowed a monstrous tub from the rental office, carted it outside and filled it with seawater. She went inside her own cottage and watched, saying nothing, as they raked charred coals from the fire pit, used dry grass and twigs as tinder, and started their own small fire. Only ripples of heat, a slight haze of smoke, rose from the sand. The sun's brilliance consumed any view of flame.

It wasn't the first time she'd seen Sam absorb himself with Hunter, but it was the first time she'd seen him use the boy to distance himself from her. He kept the boy busy snapping kindling over his knee and feeding the fire. He enlisted Hunter's help to lift the tub from the grate and douse the fire with steaming water when the crabs were done. He instructed his nephew in the messy business of cleaning, spreading newspaper over the patio and having at it, their heads together as they cracked shells and discarded gills and organs, leaving only the legs and the white flaky meat.

Aubrey retreated to her own cottage kitchen, busying her hands making salad. She'd purchased fresh vegetables at a roadside farmer's market. Arugula lettuce. An onion so moist that it dripped when she cut into it. Snow peas so fresh that they snapped when she pinched off the tips.

She went after the mixture with great zeal, tossing it with two forks, taking out her frustrations on it. *He's the one who's got the* Almighty *to talk to. You'd think he could at least explain himself to* me.

No sooner had she thought it then a shadow fell across the sink. She didn't have to turn to know someone stood in the cottage threshold. She sensed Sam there. She didn't have to look to know who stood at her door.

Self-consciously, she tucked a strand of hair behind her ear. She stared at her fingernails which, because of handling lettuce, were etched with green.

"There are only two things I've been certain of in my entire life," he said to her back. "One, I knew I was called to be a minister. Two, I wanted to find you."

Oh. *Oh.*

She turned, leaving her hands behind her spine, supporting herself against the counter.

"You should have called me about Kenneth's funeral. I could have been there for you. I wanted to be there."

So much time had passed since then.

"It was so important to me. You and Kenneth and your dad were the only things that mattered. You know I would have been there for you."

"Sam, we were both so young. I didn't know how to include you when I was trying myself to survive."

Much like I'm trying to survive now.

"I came to Piddock Beach that next summer, did you know that? I came to your house and pounded on the door. I wouldn't leave."

"Sam—"

"The neighbor, what was her name?" He frowned. "Mrs. Branton, that was it. She was making a cake. And you were just *gone.*"

She opened her mouth but could not think of a reply.

"I wanted you to marry me and I had to walk away."

"Don't," she whispered. "Don't go there, Sam. There isn't any need."

She did not know when he crossed the room. Suddenly he was standing before her, and she felt his hand on her elbow. He stood so close that she could see points of light in his eyes. She could smell the scent of him, salt in his hair and a day riding the sea on his skin. She dropped her hands from the counter, thinking she'd use them to maintain some distance. But she couldn't stop trembling.

He ran his hands up her elbows and whispered her name. Her breath caught in her throat. When she grasped the back of his neck, whorls of his hair slipped between her fingers. He pressed his forehead against hers. He touched his fingers to her throat. She leaned into him, every sinew crying out for their lives to be how they'd once been. She wanted him to kiss her.

But he did not.

He stopped himself. His hands fell away.

She felt faint with gratitude and regret. "We need to talk," she said. "The things you said, how you tried to see me, how you planned to ask me . . . to ask . . ." She stared at the floor beside his foot. "It's making me think of things I shouldn't think of."

A small silence lingered between them. "I had to tell you," he said.

"Maybe I wish you hadn't."

"What I said earlier about your father. About God's healing, plowing through something. Sometimes it's the only way."

She bit her lower lip, hating herself for the tears in her eyes.

"Your father—"

"No," she said, meeting his eyes. "It isn't my father who is hurting me."

For the second time, he whispered her name. "Where did you go that summer when you left town?"

She was shaking her head and her words came in little hiccups. "I, I can't do this," she said. When she looked up at him, she could see all the regret of the world in his eyes. "I can't, Sam." She examined the shapes in the linoleum as if they could tell her what to say. "Things aren't good right now between me and Gary. That's why this is dangerous. Being with you feels like . . . a betrayal."

Sam sat hard on the edge of the bed, as if he had collapsed.

"Do you want to know what I did the other day? I phoned my neighbor and told her how to find the key I had left under the mat for the housekeeper. I spent twenty minutes giving her directions so she could dig through Hannah's toy box, looking for a blue stuffed elephant with one eye gone. When she found it, she drove to the post office to pay and have it overnighted to my daughter. 'Oh, yes, and make sure you get the insurance,' I told her. 'After all this, don't run any risk of it getting lost in the mail.' Thirty bucks for postage, when Hannah could have something new for *ten*."

The sun had moved toward the west outside. Clouds pillared above the sea, which would make for a spec-

225

tacular sunset. Hazy light poured through the open door.

"It's not the practical thing, is it?" Aubrey began to stir the salad in sharp, shaky motions. "But that's how it works. Even a four year old knows. You can't exchange one thing for another."

Aubrey could see her reflection in the faucet. She could also see it in the droplet of water growing from the spout, not yet heavy enough to fall. When she picked up the salad bowl to carry it to the refrigerator, she felt as if she carried her life in her own shaking hands, so easily dropped, so easily broken.

She said, "I only want to be here with you."

"Aubrey. Don't . . ."

"Gary is in alcohol treatment. He hasn't been emotionally present in our marriage for a long time."

I've used you, Sam. Used what you used to feel for me to reassure myself. To numb myself. She slid the bowl in the refrigerator and turned toward him. She knelt in front of him, her heart aching. *I've used you the same way Gary uses alcohol.* "For the life of me, I can't think what would orchestrate such a thing," she said. "That I would run away to Piddock Beach and find you here."

There. She'd said it. She looked up at him again as he raked his fingers through his hair, and she saw he'd turned a ghastly pale.

"Oh, Aub," he whispered. "I was only thinking of my own heart. I'm so sorry. I pushed it too far."

"But don't you see, Sam? I *wanted* you to push. I wanted to feel—" She stopped, buried her face in her

226

palms, then gazed up again. "—I wanted to feel the way I used to feel. I wanted it to be easy again." And then, "Only it was never easy, was it?"

"No." He combed his fingers through his hair again. "It wasn't, Aubrey. Not even then. The thing I remember most was having to tell you good-bye."

CHAPTER TWENTY-ONE

When they thought back to it later, neither Sam nor Aubrey could tell when the shouting on the beach began. The patio door was open to the sunset. Sam grew aware of the fracas bit by bit. Suddenly, he noticed the loud, angry voices. He recognized the familiar barking of a dog.

He rushed out into the evening light, "Ginny!" expecting to see her splashing in the swells, her tongue lolling to one side. But when Sam saw her, she was springing around something in a circle, her paws flopping, her ears streaming gleefully. When he called her name again, she didn't even slow down.

Sam shaded his eyes against the sunset. When he heard Hunter's frantic shouting, Sam realized something was wrong. He began to run toward the sea.

At the point where foam slipped onto shore, the harbor seal had deposited her baby again. The animal lay in the sand like a smooth rock, entirely motionless, still and sleek. Its head rested on the beach. Its eyes were trusting pools of light, watching Hunter.

Even from this distance, Sam could see tears

streaming down his nephew's face as a crowd pressed in toward the seal. He saw a trail in the sand and realized the seal was bleeding from a gash in its side.

The seal had strayed from its protected place and it lay in a heap upon the sand, in the middle of a crowded section of beach. One of Hunter's friends who built the bonfire darted close enough to jab it with a stick. Ginny twisted and leapt, beside herself at the scent of blood. She danced and leapt. Hunter tried to hold her at bay with his command, but it was no use. If Ginny came close to the injured creature, she would do it harm. A dog is bred to hunt in the wild. Sam had once seen her jaws snap the neck of a duck.

"Hunter!" Sam shouldered past strangers, or maybe they parted in front of him, he couldn't be sure. He was suddenly as frightened for the seal as Hunter was. "Stand back, people. Please." Still, he shoved his way through. It must have been his voice working, but he never felt himself speak. "You will harm the animal."

Like a featured attraction in the center of a ring, Hunter had grabbed a sharp, forked length of wood. It was wet and, as he used it as a foil against the dog and the others who were coming too close, thick pearls of water flew through the air. Later, Sam would learn that it must have been Ginny who first discovered the seal. She must have alerted everyone to its presence by her hopping and barking. Tourists gathered to touch and prod. The wound might have come from broken glass, a prodding stick, or a dog's teeth. They would never be sure.

Sam remembered his cell phone in his pocket. *Ridiculous to do this!* Sam thought as he dialed 911, the only thing he knew to do. He expected the dispatcher to hang up on him, but she didn't. She patched him through immediately to a marine wildlife service.

From another world, Sam heard himself describing the location of the cottages. They told him to keep the seal safe from further harm. "We're sending a truck." He could hear computer keys clicking in the background. "Because of the traffic, I can't estimate when we'll arrive."

Sam folded his phone and shoved it inside his rear pocket. "Buddy. It's okay." But Hunter had gone beyond comprehending faces and voices and instructions. Sam was on the wrong end of the driftwood. Hunter's muscles bulged beneath his T-shirt sleeves as he fought off his uncle. Sam tried to shield himself with the heels of his hands, but Hunter was striking blindly.

"Kid, it's me. It's okay."

Hunter took two more well-aimed jabs before he recognized his uncle. He stared, surprised, for a moment. The stick angled into the sand. Sam gripped Hunter's shoulders and drew the boy against him. Even then, they both understood that the seal would be hauled away.

Through the jostle, Sam saw Aubrey wrest Ginny by the collar. He shot her a look of gratitude as she led the dog to the cottage. "The seal is injured." Sam's voice boomed like it was directed from a pulpit. Its authority surprised even him. "If you want to save its life, you

229

must disband." Even as Sam said the words, the wildlife truck topped a hillock, rattling toward them, crushing wild roses and agate beneath its tires. The scent, which Sam would never forget, was a sweet mixture of diesel and roses and crushed sandstone and oil.

The wail began deep in Hunter's throat. He struggled against his uncle again, wielding the stick. "It's okay, Hunter," Sam said. "It's okay."

Only, it wasn't.

They both understood that a mother would return to the sand to retrieve her young, and that the young, innocent thing would no longer be there.

When Sam grabbed the end of Hunter's flailing weapon, splinters pierced deep in his skin. When Hunter finally realized he could stop swinging, he dropped the makeshift sword onto the ground. Sam gathered his sister's son into his arms.

Most of the bystanders on the beach had slipped away by the time the wildlife officer had examined the animal. All this time, the creature has never taken its eyes from Hunter. Sam dropped one of his arms and used all of his force to propel the boy forward along the beach. As they lifted the newborn seal into a net and wet it down with seawater, tears rolled down the boy's face.

He struggled against his uncle one last time, lofting three halfhearted swings into the air. "Nothing's going to be okay."

"Hunter."

"No."

Their feet dug into the sand, making them stumble against each other. It was tough going. They were both gasping by the time they slowed and Sam released him.

"There's nothing I can say," Sam said. "There's nothing I can do to make it any better."

"Don't you think I *know* that?" Hunter bent to catch his breath, his hands on his knees. "My dad's dead. Mom's a mess. I crashed your car. Your church sent you away. And you didn't even want me here! How can you pretend?"

Hearing it listed out was like getting pummeled in the gut. "You're right. A lot of things are bad right now."

"Mr. Ransom came to the house. He told Mom that if you stay the way you are, they don't want you anymore." Hunter enjoyed saying it, Sam could tell. Sometimes it felt like if you lashed out at others, some of the pain would leave your heart with the lashing. Sam met his stare. Sam saw anger in Hunter's eyes, almost threatening, but underneath the anger, there was confusion.

"Hunter—"

"I wrecked your car."

"You will pay me for the car. You had no right to do that."

"I stole it out of your garage."

"That doesn't make me not love you."

Hunter and Sam tromped through the sand the same way they were tromping on each other's hearts, getting farther and farther from the water line. They stumbled through a tangle of driftwood logs. Sam sat down hard on one of them. He pulled his nephew down at his side.

"I heard you tell Mom that she was the one who had to take care of me—that you didn't want to," Hunter repeated, the same line he'd used to condemn himself before.

Sam's pants were dusted with sand. "Things have turned out differently than I thought they would."

He could see that Hunter's anger had finally begun to drain. Sam broke off a piece of driftwood lying at their feet—part of an old, dead limb—and began scratching patterns in the crusted sand beside his feet. Hunter said in a choked voice, "It might take me half my *life* to pay you back, but I'm going to. I'll get a job when we get home."

Sam and Aubrey stopped at the chainlink gate meant to keep visitors from the pier. Below, they could see the harbor licking the prow of the old boat. The anchor dangled from a rusty chain. A thick layer of salt encrusted the windows. Walt McCart must not have washed them in a very long time. The painted name across the stern of the vessel had worn until it was barely legible.

No-Nonsense II.

At first glance, the deck looked to be deserted. But Sam glimpsed the man sitting on a stool off to one side. He had a wild look about him that Sam didn't remember. He looked as if he'd just blown in from a storm. His sandals were cracked, his feet planted wide with defiance.

Mr. McCart's grizzled beard made him appear old for

his years. Sam couldn't be sure whether his high color was because of sunburn or drink. Sam realized that moment that he might have been wrong. This wouldn't be as simple as calling to him and asking to be let in. Aubrey touched his arm. "Sam? Do you see him? Now do you understand?"

While driving Aubrey over here this morning, Sam had felt certainty instead of fear. He had felt peace instead of worry. He understood that, during the past few days in Piddock Beach, something had refreshed his heart and made it change.

Be my first love, Father, he'd prayed. *Help me minister to the one I have always put before you.*

Still, even knowing about Gary's drinking, Sam couldn't access the sorrow in Aubrey's eyes. It seemed to reach into the depths of her soul. He had to make this statement. "I never understood why your father gave all the credit to your brother and never any to you."

She lowered her gaze to her fingers, which were wrapped around a link in the gate. "The night before he left for Vietnam he said, 'If I get out of this town, I'll be out of Dad's hair. He'll stop thinking I'm the only kid he's got.' Then he said, 'I can promise you that, Aubrey.'"

"He shouldn't have made promises he couldn't keep." She pressed her forehead against the gate. "I always wondered if you came that summer." When she shut her eyes, he could scarcely bear it.

Sam stared at the dilapidated boat as it rocked in its mooring.

"You always loved me, Sam. And my father never did."

In the distance, the man sat on the stool, listing with the boat as it rode the swells. A battered, stained fishing cap sat on McCart's knees.

"You have a father who loves you, Aubrey. Not your earthly father. A heavenly one."

"Some good that does. I wouldn't even know how that feels."

He tucked her hand over his elbow, compelled to pursue this. The soil of her spirit had been tilled; he could not turn away.

"What do you want out of your life, Aubrey? All the times we've talked, you've never said."

She opened her eyes and lifted her head. "I want to have a family that doesn't fall apart."

"You have a God who will always think you're amazing, a savior who died for you." He moved a tendril of her hair behind her ear. "He sees you as everything good you can be."

She was still gripping the gate with both hands. He was surprised, suddenly, to realize she was wearing a wedding ring. She'd caught him looking at it. "I still love Gary. I love the man he is when he doesn't drink. Weren't you going to ask me about that, Sam?"

He said nothing.

"I put the ring away for a little while."

She reached for the latch on the gate and opened it. For the first time, Sam realized it hadn't been locked.

"He took me to an aunt's house that summer." She

held the gate open. "My mother's sister. He never wanted me to live with him again."

"Were you—?" He studied a cloud above her head. Above him, seagulls bantered in the sky. He hesitated, not knowing how to ask this. "Your neighbor told me there might be a child."

Her smile did not reach her eyes. "That's what *always* goes around town, isn't it?"

"Maybe," he admitted. "But if that isn't it, what is it that your father blames you for?"

"Maybe he just blames me for not being my brother."

Walt McCart leaned slightly toward them as they neared, his ragged brows furrowed, obviously uncomfortable at being approached. It the brief moment after Sam stepped aboard and offered his hand, Walt's eyes seemed to be the only entrance into the past. Although they had aged, they were still familiar, pale blue, sun-faded, the color of the ocean in a glass. These were kind eyes whose owner offered him the paradise of fighting salmon being reeled in with a rod.

The fishing hat fell to the deck when Walt stood, and Sam shook the man's hand. "I'm Sam Tibbits. My dad and I used to fish at your place."

But Walt McCart wasn't peering at Sam anymore. He was eyeing his daughter, who had also come aboard. He stood from the stool so fast that it toppled over. He unknotted the stern rope from its mooring and let it fall into a coil on the deck.

Walt picked up his hat and dusted it against his discolored pants. He yanked it onto his balding head.

"Dad. Don't."

"I told you not to come back here again. Didn't I say that?"

"Daddy," she cried. "I'm your daughter. I can't help that I'm not Kenneth. Please tell me why you won't have a thing to do with me."

"Get off my boat."

"Why won't you look at me?"

Sam said, "Aubrey—"

"Why did you sell your boats and send me away when we needed each other most?" Aubrey squeezed her knuckles against her mouth. "Won't you look at me and see what you have instead of what you don't?"

There was a moment when it seemed like the world held its breath. Walt reached for the throttle. If he started the boat now, they would both be thrown overboard. But he didn't. He stayed his hand.

"There was a bee in your lifejacket on the day your mother died. She bent to help you because you had gotten stung. She never saw the boom swing toward her."

"Daddy. I . . ."

McCart gazed past the harbor's mouth to the buoys that marked the open sea. "I've never been able to be fair to you, Aubrey. You and I both know that. I can't help myself, no matter how hard I try."

Chapter Twenty-Two

Sam held the car door open as Aubrey loaded her duffel bag into the back seat. The warning bell buzzed for having the key in the ignition, the door open. Neither of them noticed the painful pinging.

"I have to do this," she said, staring down at Sam's hand on the door. "The kids need me to stand beside their father in respect, not to run away in shame."

The door handle felt hot beneath his hand.

"If I hide it from them any longer, I give Gary's struggle power over all of us."

"I'm proud of you, Aubrey."

"Are you?" He could tell by her eyes that she was hungry to hear it.

"Yes."

She pressed her fingers to his lips. "I'm not willing to lose everything to bitterness the way my own dad did."

"Maybe he won't have to give up everything," Sam said. "Don't give up with him. Keep trying."

"Oh, Sam."

"It was good to see you again," he said gently.

She answered, "It was good for me, too."

In order to go forward, to go ahead with what the Father intended for their lives, neither of them wanted anything left behind.

When Aubrey gripped his wrist and raised her eyes to his, he closed his eyes for a moment. He held his breath, feeling the warmth of her heart, the warmth of her hand.

He knew this would be the last time they would ever see each other.

"Aubrey McCart." He said her name one final time. And they both knew that, although some parts might not be easy, they would follow their journeys through to completion.

I give Aubrey to you, Lord. Heal her marriage, Father. I've held on to the dream of her for way too long.

"Go find your life, Sam."

"I will. I promise."

"Good."

"I'll be praying for you and Gary. I also promise you that."

He let go of the car and she gripped the lapels of his shirt. "I believe you." She smiled. "After all these years, I believe that you are one who will keep your promises."

Her CD case was tented upside down on her front seat. He saw her lips trembling. He knew then that they could put the moment off no longer. All had been said, and done. He covered her hands with his own. She gripped his shirt tighter. He never wanted to let her go.

"Thank you," she mouthed to him. He could see flecks of light in her clear, green eyes. He remembered once how she'd told him about the green phosphorescence in the sea.

When she stood on tiptoe to kiss him, he lowered his mouth to hers. He could feel her heart hammering against their joined hands. Sam kept her against him a little longer than he thought proper. But this needed to make up for a lost summer, a hurting, confused boy, a daughter who never knew her mother. He thought, *This, then, is the way we will leave it. The kiss we share will be a kiss of good-bye.* After he released her, she fumbled with the key. He took one last glimpse of all that blustery, free hair before she shut the door.

By the time Aubrey backed out of the cottage parking lot, the sun was glinting on the window and he couldn't see her face. He stepped out into the street to watch her go. He watched until her car became a speck.

The windows glinted once more as she turned into the distance. He kept waving for a long time, even though he could see her no more.

The candles inside the church in Piddock Beach had all been lit for the service. The smell of vanilla permeated the air and the ivory wax cast a warm, living glow. The pipe organ played as worshippers filed inside, rustled hymnbooks, and found a place to sit.

Outside along the water, a squall had begun. Rain peppered the ground, leaving pocked holes in the sand. Whitecaps tossed buoys at the mouth of the bay. The whale watching excursions had been cancelled for the day.

The gray clouds darkened the church's square-cut stones, the granite headstones in the cemetery and the shadows along the twin steeples. Inside the sanctuary, as Pastor Solomon Fraser stepped in to start today's sermon, the stained-glass windows looked flat and dull;

the pictures of seagulls and lighthouses could be seen only faintly.

Sam didn't know why he'd felt such a need to come today. Perhaps he came to mourn his lost love of a girl, perhaps he came in thanksgiving because he had discovered his lost love of God, perhaps both.

Hunter had not wanted to come with him. Sam had planned to leave directly after Solomon Fraser's message. But a torrent of rain had started outside. Worshipers sheltered themselves in the front foyer, not yet ready to dart out into the rain. The front foyer was a bottleneck.

Sam was inching toward a side exit when he saw Solomon moving toward him through the crowd. He smiled, nodded his head.

"I'm so glad to see you. I'd been hoping for a way to talk to you." Solomon offered his hand. "Would you come to my study for a minute? This way please."

Sam followed, his curiosity getting the best of him.

The room they entered was lined with heavy walnut shelves, much different from the study that Sam kept elsewhere. The downpour outside cast each item on Solomon's desk in a cool, pewter hue.

Sam made himself comfortable in the wingback chair that faced the desk.

"I did not tell you this when you visited before." Solomon shrugged out of his robe and hung in on a hatrack beside him. "I am retiring in a few months. It is time for this, and I am ready. But still, as you must imagine, it is . . . difficult."

Sam felt his throat working. He did not know where this might lead.

"It is unusual to do things this way, I know. They have started building a search committee. And, of course, the position must be filled with someone of proper training and vision."

"I understand."

"This is a church any pastor would wish for." Solomon positioned himself in his chair and braided his fingers behind his head. "This congregation makes everyone welcome. They are used to visitors on the beach; they make everyone welcome."

Sam thought he must have gone pale. Solomon stopped and asked if he needed a drink of water.

"I'm fine." Sam shook his head.

"It is a church where the call to reach out for Christ is taken quite seriously."

Sam gripped the handles on the chair.

"I know this might be dangling a carrot in front of you, but I don't want to go further without your permission. I wondered if you would allow me to submit your name."

He was clinging to the chair so tightly that his knuckles had gone white.

"I sensed something in you from the very first time I saw you, Sam. And I know that you have an affinity for the area."

"Solomon," he choked out the words, considering the offer earnestly. "You will never know how honored I am." A spark had begun to take hold inside him that could not be held back. "I understand what it is like to leave a beloved congregation in the hands of another."

"Well? What do you think?" Solomon tilted his head in expectation of an answer.

And Sam said, "The Piddock Beach chapter of my life is over, Solomon. What awaits me is back home."

Aubrey could have chosen to drive straight down the coast, or she could have turned inland. The coast offered more tranquil beauty, a longer time of contemplation, more challenging driving. The highway, which took her smack-dab down the spine of Oregon and California, would carry her south to Emily's in half the time. Aubrey chose the more scenic route, the one with hairpin turns and blind corners, not because she wasn't anxious to arrive at her destination, but because the view pleased her, the glorious heights as the road threaded its way out of the trees, the vast contour of sand etching the coast, the commas of whitecaps stretching farther than she could ever see.

She followed a route not so different from the route she had followed in her own life. It afforded her the time to think about herself, and her earthly father Walt McCart, and her heavenly Father, who loved her above all things. Aubrey was able to pull off and park the car often, to stand atop the headlands, overlooking what felt like the edge of the world. As she gazed over the panorama of sky and dune and coastal forest, she knew she would return again to her father's boat. She would return with courage to the slip where Walt McCart's boat was moored. She would say, *I choose not to pull away from you, Father. I am available to you when you are ready. Sam has showed this to me. With God's help, the wound you've carried doesn't have to be a wound in me, too.*

That would be a healing for another day. But for now, Aubrey knew where this drive must take her. Not to confront her past, but to secure her future.

Aubrey spent one restless night in a mission hotel near San Luis Obispo, waking often, praying, checking the clock. She rose before dawn, grabbing breakfast at McDonald's, balancing the paper cup of coffee between her knees.

When she steered inland toward The Five and began to fight traffic in earnest, cars zipped past her on both sides, boxing her in. But she kept her speed steady. She didn't feel hemmed in. She felt waveswept and wind-blown, refreshed, born anew, free.

She parked in front of Emily's house and took two deep breaths, leaning her head against the seat, admitting to herself that she was afraid. It would be so easy to start the engine again and flee. But to hide the truth about Gary from the children, though she'd thought she'd been hiding it in love, could be to buffer them from the very power in the family that God wanted them to grow accustomed to and expect.

She needed only to stand beside her husband and define healthy boundaries and let him know she loved him and was proud of him, that she opened her heart to how he wanted to heal so he could lead his family.

She could do this. She could.
No, she could not. Only God could.

Because of Sam Tibbits, she had begun to rely on a Holy God who wanted to grow her by playing out an adventure.

And, oh, how Aubrey had always loved adventures!

Emily's screen door banged open and out jumped Hannah, her little legs pumping, her limbs flying akimbo. "Mom! What are you doing here?"

"I've come to take you home."

Hannah looked around. "Where's Daddy?"

"We'll pick him up soon. In a little while. But the rest of us need to be together before that."

I will never leave you or forsake you.

"Aunt Emily is taking us to get *hamgurbers,*" Hannah chirped like a little bird.

"Really?"

She lofted Hannah into her arms, assaulted by the chubby little limbs that encircled her like a vice. Years later, Aubrey would remember this moment not in tight-knit details, but in small, precious blurs: the others spilling into Emily's yard to welcome her; the brilliant turquoise of Channing's new gypsy skirt; the shape of Billy's hands as he leapt to catch the lowest branch of a tree. She would always remember the musty smell of Hannah's hair as Hannah smattered her face with kisses, Billy's socks wrinkled around his ankles. So much innocence, Aubrey wanted to cry. And she would remember Channing's eyes, the same gray hue as an encroaching squall.

Aubrey let Hannah slide to the ground so she could embrace her oldest daughter. When she did, their heights were evenly matched, shoulder to shoulder, ear to ear. When had Channing grown so tall?

Her mind had played a trick on her. When she'd imagined Channing coming to meet her, she'd pictured a more spindly girl, not quite reaching her shoulders. Aubrey had forgotten to expect a young woman instead of a child. When they hugged, Channing felt sturdy and strong in her arms. Channing looked into Aubrey's eyes with great intent, as if she looked much farther than she could see. Aubrey knew by her expression that Channing understood things were not exactly as they should be.

There was a long silence between mother and daughter in which Aubrey realized the truth. *I'm not hiding anything from her. Channing understands about her father.*

Aubrey told the three of them quietly, "Tomorrow morning, I'll take you home."

CHAPTER TWENTY-THREE

Just after lunch, Mary Grace Pokorny pivoted toward her computer at Covenant Heights and began compiling the calendar for the upcoming month. The items had come to her in various shapes and forms, some via phone calls, some via e-mail, some via Post-it notes. Choir practice, she typed. Wednesday at 7 p.m.

Mary Grace's fingers paused on the keys. She stared

at the screen, seeing nothing. *Oh, Pastor Tibbits. If only you could see what's happening here.*

Three gold frames lay at various angles on the work-station beside her. This afternoon, with her other responsibilities out of the way, she would frame Pastor Tibbits' theology diplomas. She'd discovered them in a stack of folders she'd been asked to sort through after the interim pastor arrived. And Sam Tibbits' leave-taking had made her notice something. Along with the rows of C.S. Lewis books and his tattered copy of the *Disciples' Study Bible*, he'd surrounded himself with mementos of his congregation, a picture of Brenda and Joe's wedding, a child's crayon-scribbled message that read, "Your the best, Kelly," a cross of burled maple that Ian Barker had carved for him, a nativity scene that Dottie Graham had fashioned from cornhusks.

Nothing in the room bespoke the man's stature and education. Instead, he'd chosen to surround himself with reminders of those he loved.

Mary Grace had taken one look at the heavy parch-ment diplomas, the gilded seminary crests, the ornate letters that spelled MASTER OF DIVINITY, DOCTORATE OF MINISTRY, and thought, *if Pastor Tibbits had a woman in his life, she'd make certain these saw the light of day!*

She rose from her computer and absently fingered the hem of her sleeve. Covenant Heights had fared satis-factorily without their regular pastor; she could not grumble about that. The interim's sermons provoked hearty discussion. The women's covenant group had started another Beth Moore Bible Study. Lester Kraft had donated a renovated eBay telescope for the youth group's auction.

But no one could have told her how much she would miss Sam Tibbits.

She'd catch herself glancing up when the door opened, expecting to see his face. She'd catch herself conjecturing at odd times, wondering what he might be doing. She'd catch herself thinking, *oh, just wait until I tell Pastor Tibbits about this!*

Her cell phone awaited her beside the cubicles of yellow paper she used for Covenant Heights' newsletters. Even as she reached for the phone for the umpteenth time and searched for his number, Mary Grace felt her cheeks color. Did she dare do it? Oh, but it would never do to bother him! Confound her fair coloring, her red hair! If anyone saw her this minute, they'd think she'd swallowed a firecracker.

Mary Grace dialed and pressed the phone to her ear. Too late, she almost wished he wouldn't answer. She rehearsed a message as she listened to the ringing on the other end. *No need to call back,* she would sing lightly. *Just wanted to share the news.* Her heart caught in her throat when she heard the click on the other end, followed by a dull roar.

"Hello?"

"Pastor Tibbits?"

"Mary Grace? Is it you?"

"It is."

"How are you? Everything okay?"

"Everything's fine. I wanted to . . . Where *are* you,

Pastor Tibbits? You sound like you're in a car wash."

She heard him chuckle before he said somewhat proudly, "I'm somewhere in eastern Nebraska." She heard the smile in his voice. "We've decided to head home."

"Oh." Mary Grace sank into her chair. "You shouldn't have answered . . . I shouldn't have called . . . Well, I didn't know you would be *driving.*"

"It's fine. I'm not behind the wheel. It's good to hear you! Hold on." He said something to someone over the roar, instructing someone to watch the speed limit and exit at a gas station in Scottsbluff. She heard someone close a window, and he returned. "Can you hear now? I certainly can."

"I can," she told him. "Thank you."

"My nephew's driving. We've been trading off. He's doing a good job handling this car."

She decided he sounded different, settled, satisfied. She squashed her cell against her head with both hands, heard him say, "Mary Grace."

"I have . . . I mean . . . I called because I have news."

"I hope the news is good!" As if he wouldn't be expecting anything else.

"Your friend Kil has come to church every Sunday."

"I didn't—" The line roared with sounds, none of which were Sam Tibbits.

"Are you there, Pastor Tibbits? Did I lose you?"

"Well, how about that?"

Ah, Mary Grace thought. She'd done the right thing, telling him. How she enjoyed the disbelief in his voice!

"You're surprised, aren't you? Wait until you hear the rest of it. Ted and Mary Barker, Ian's parents, heard the story about him losing his dog Bench. They went to the animal adoption center and paid fees for a new dog."

"But another dog," he said. "Kil has trouble taking care of hims—"

"Cutest little thing, you should see it. It's got a brown circle over one eye. Kil's named this one *Sofa*. Says he's always wanted a sofa.

"Kil keeps coming, don't you see? He doesn't know what happened in the meeting. Some make a wide berth around him but others make him welcome. The whole thing has taken on a life of its own.

"Ted found him a job, that's the other thing. Kil's stacking supplies at the animal adoption center. He's taking donations for the animals."

So much for the man who'd made speaking his life's work. "Well, how about that," he repeated. It seemed he had lost his vocabulary.

"Pastor Tibbits?" she called over the line. "Is that all you have to say?"

"Oh, Mary Grace," he said. "So much has happened." Then, "You're the first besides Brenda to know. Will you let Grant Ransom know that I'll be in town tomorrow?"

Even though he wasn't employed by Covenant Heights when he arrived home, Sam found plenty to do. He painted the trim at Brenda's house. He took Hunter to a Christian rap concert and out for a hamburger so they could have long talks about the words. One evening, he showed Hunter one of his old journals in which he'd written about Aubrey. He told his nephew how much writing had helped him survive when he was hurting. Before Sam left Brenda's, he was rewarded with a hip-hop beat resounding from the computer in Hunter's room.

"Thanks a *lot* for the noise," his sister said.

"My therapy bill will be in the mail," he teased her.

When he opened the door a crack to tell Hunter he'd see him later, the beat was blaring. Hunter had his head bent over his desk, scribbling lyrics on a crumpled piece of notebook paper.

Sam spent one day golfing with his father. He spent a day at the feed store, encouraging Kil in his new job and letting Ginny have a sniff of Sofa, Kil's new dog. And every afternoon for ten days, Sam sat in the wicker chair in his mother's room, where he could see straight out the window to the green oval of lawn.

One visit, he described Hunter's antics as he'd run along the shore with twine in his hand, trying to keep the brilliant trapezoid kite aloft in the wind. Another day, he told her how the Sunset Vue Motor Court had been sold and their favorite stretch of beach had been converted to houses of various styles and sizes. He described to her at least three different sunsets. He brought his guitar one day and sang her a song.

Through all this, his mother sat in the opposite chair, smiling politely at him, the way she'd smile at a some-what-annoying stranger. The nurse combed her hair every morning and, in the diffused sunlight that fell through the narrow blinds, it shone like spun silver. Sam told her story after story about Piddock Beach while he counseled himself to remain patient.

"You remember how the seals sunned themselves on the rocks, Mom? Hunter came upon one and knew not to stand too close." He reminded her how good the clams tasted when they were steamed and dipped in melted butter. He described the color of the water and the smell of the sea.

Finally, disappointed, he rose from his chair and kissed her good-bye on the cheek. While her face was lifted toward his, she asked, "Do you remember how perfect the shells could be, Sam? So small, with ridges as intricate as cake icing. Oh, didn't we have so much fun?"

Watching Hunter count beats and create his songs made Sam revisit the idea of writing in his own journals again. Of course, it would never do to add entries to something he had already started. He had new ideas about things and therefore he needed the right sort of book. Something leather, with papers of substance, something that felt weighty when he carried it.

Which is how he ended up on a particular aisle at Staples, unable to decide between the three choices in his hands. He glanced up when he heard someone muttering over the envelopes across the way.

"Mary Grace."

She was pushing around reams of printer paper in her

cart, an assortment of colored push pins, an automatic pencil sharpener that resembled a NASA space probe.

"How are you?"

"I'd be much better if I could find those envelopes with the windows, the ones with the sticky gum on the flap. You don't see those over there, do you? With all the letters I have to get out, I don't want to have to lick."

"I always think about Florida when I see you, did you know that?"

"Oh." She straightened, smoothed her sweater over her hips with her hands. "Thank you."

Silence. He couldn't think of anything more to say. He, Sam Tibbits, who made a career out of speaking.

She shouldered her purse. It banged against her side where her waist nipped in. The florescent bulbs buzzed overhead and a loudspeaker blared. At the front of the store, a harried cashier stuffed items in a plastic bag.

"I never thanked you for the telephone call," he said. "The day Hunter and I were driving home."

"Oh," she said, sounding flustered. "I thought it might be the right thing to do."

"You encouraged me." He thumbed through the pages of one of the journals in his hand. "I knew I was supposed to return. I didn't know what everyone here would think of it. Your words gave me hope."

"Well." She sounded pleased. "You're welcome."

"And I have another question to ask."

"You do?"

"Yes."

"Go ahead."

252

"A funny question, actually." Sam suddenly realized he was nervous. Might be better if he bided his time for a while. It was too late now. "It's something that might make you laugh."

"It might," she encouraged him, "but you could try me."

"Do people at Covenant Heights ever try to set you up on dates?"

"Oh, all the time!" She gestured toward the ground. "You should have heard them call when Wyatt Hanbury started coming to church. The phone rang off the hook. They wouldn't leave me alone for days."

Well. Sam selected the journal he wanted and put the others decisively aside. "Wyatt Hanbury, hum?"

"I know." When she blushed, even the tips of her ears turned red. "Isn't that funny?"

"I always wondered—" Sam examined rolls of Scotch tape as if he'd never seen such things before. "—if anyone suggested that you might go out with *me*."

She seemed interested in the envelopes again.

"What I mean is, there is an antique car rally at the Amana Colonies next month. I'd like to drive over for the day, see some more Iowa farm country I haven't had the time to see. I was wondering if you'd like to do that, too. With me, I mean. I, well, I know Hanbury is a nice fellow. But, for you, I had someone other than Wyatt Hanbury in mind."

CHAPTER TWENTY-FOUR

When the cell phone rang and Sam heard Libby Kraft's voice, he knew something must be terribly wrong with her husband, Lester. Libby struggled to speak as she tried to explain.

"It's, it's Lester, Pastor Tibbits. Please help us. We need you to come over right away."

"Libby." He kept his voice even, trying to keep her calm. Even as he spoke to her, he found himself praying. *They need what* you *can give them, Father, not what* I *can. Help me be an instrument of your peace.* "Can you tell me what's happened?"

"He was in his truck, backing out of his driveway and he didn't see anyone. He didn't—didn't know."

"Libby?" Sam felt the wrench in his own heart, knew he was stepping into an impossible situation. "Was someone hurt?"

"Our little Casey. Our little boy."

Sam's heart sank. For a moment, he couldn't place the child she mentioned. His heart lodged in his throat when he realized. Of course he knew. Lester and Libby's four-year-old nephew. "Is he . . . ?"

"Oh, Sam."

"Libby, is the boy alive?"

The choked sobs on the other end of the line spoke the grievous words that Libby could not. Hurt for his friend Lester slammed Sam like a fist. Even as he balanced the phone beneath his chin, Sam shrugged into his jacket. The leatherette cover on the Bible he grabbed had been worn creased and broken like an old shoe. With all of his being, Sam begged his Lord to be present and sustain the Kraft family. He knew exactly where he belonged.

The interim pastor at Covenant Heights, Reverend Jack Jensen, was the one who helped Casey Boyd's parents grieve. He told the little boy's mother that it was okay to be angry at God. He helped the child's father erect a fountain at the end of their driveway from copper tubing and pieces of cement. He also led a candlelight vigil on the second night for the families and neighbors who wanted to do something, but who could not think of anything that would help.

Pastor Sam Tibbits sat with the Krafts at their home, about four blocks over. No one came to light candles in Lester's driveway or to sing songs or to cry. No one brought lasagnas or cookies or said, "I've stopped by to give you a hug." But Libby and Lester were not alone during the darkest hour of their lives. Sam sat beside them. They cried together. They searched the Scriptures together as the heavens darkened and evening drained from the sky.

Shortly after midnight, during the wee hours of the morning on August 14, the interim pastor phoned Sam. "I am here with Casey Boyd's parents," Reverend Jensen explained. "You are the man who has been with the Kraft family. You are the man who can pull the community together during the tragedy. Everyone I've spoken to agrees on this. The Boyds would like for you to preach their little boy's funeral service."

As the afternoon sun mantled the Iowa hills, a person could almost pretend it was waves in the ocean rolling, rolling. Sam leaned against the church's stairwell, his head against the rough plaster. His eyes were so gritty from lack of sleep he felt like someone had thrown sand into them.

He might have had a hundred better reasons to step into the pulpit than this one. The funeral service for little Casey Boyd was about to begin. The coffee was perking in the silver urn in the hospitality center and goodies were being laid out by members of the women's ministry. Sam struggled with his nerves as he slipped into his robe, draped the stole across his shoulders. He'd never guessed he'd feel this nervous! He ran his tongue against the roof of his mouth, which had gone bone-dry.

If he'd thought stepping in front of his congregation again would feel mundane or ordinary, he couldn't have been more wrong. His heart marched in his chest. His throat felt like it might never work again.

Ian Barker bustled around him, attaching a microphone to Sam's robe. Ian tapped the microphone with his finger, making certain it was turned on. "You're all set."

Thanks, Sam mouthed.

He coughed into the circle of his fist. He crossed the chancel, stepped forward, and gripped the sides of the pulpit. When he offered words of welcome, Sam could hear the shake in his voice. When he saw Casey's mother reach for Libby's hand, he felt his heart breaking in love. When he began to speak in earnest, he completely disregarded his notes.

Sam spoke of grief as he caught Lester's gaze. He spoke of tragedy, of a young child whose life had ended much too soon. That completed, Sam spoke of something that could never be explained away by cosmology research or quantum physics or any other scientific theory. He spoke of forgiveness. Of one human to another. Of one to oneself. And, of God to man.

CHAPTER TWENTY-FIVE

When Mary Grace arrived at Covenant Heights, she could see lights already on in the room where they would meet. She hurried to the office and grabbed the agendas which she'd typed earlier in the day. As she carried the papers to the conference room and placed one in front of each person's chair, the humid August air pressed against her lungs like a heavy hand.

The board members and deacons entered the room with wariness, afraid they were in for a quarrel. Dave Hawthorne gripped his chair as if he were at the fair waiting for the Wildcat Coaster to jerk forward. John McKinley read over his agenda with the same fascination he might have for a manual explaining how to build an engine. Grant Ransom adjusted his position at the table with both hands, his eyes darting from Dave's upper lip to John's necktie to the top of Mary Grace's head.

"This meeting is called to order," Grant said, looking almost ill. Mary Grace began scribbling notes by hand, making scratching noises as she formed the letters with her pen. *Whatever happens here is in the Lord's hands, not mine.* In spite of her apparent ease, she felt like the floor might fall away, that she might be about to fall fifty feet.

The group sat like stones during the approval of the minutes. They had no comment during the treasurer's report. They did not shift in their chairs during the introduction of old business. They did not frown at their reflections in the polished tabletop. They did not tap their toes in frustration or rake their fingers through their hair.

"Next item on the agenda," Grant said as he stared at his notes, "is reinstatement for Pastor Samuel Tibbits." No one else initiated discussion on this matter. They deferred to Grant, to hear what he might have to say.

Mary Grace laid down her pen, certain Grant would see the tremor in her hand. Apart from a sharp and perhaps too hasty glance at the man who sat across from her, she did not give herself away.

Dave Hawthorne was first to pick up his water glass and take a sip. After an extremely loud swallow, he said, "Three days ago, I would have told you I believe Grant owes the pastor an apology. But now I believe I'm wrong."

No. Mary Grace flipped to the next page of her note-book and stared unseeingly at the ruled lines. *Please let them see.*

"I believe Grant isn't the only one to blame." Dave steepled his fingers and pressed them beneath his nose. "I believe all of us share an equal amount of the blame."

Grant's hand hit his agenda. "Now, see here. We all agreed Sam needed the rest."

"Yes." John leaned forward. "But some of our motivations were different."

Dave examined his thumbnail. "Ministers can sometimes create enemies by the faithful discharge of their duties. A great many of them labor in vain."

Grant shoved himself away from the table. John held up a hand to stop him. "I agree that Pastor Tibbits needed a rest. But we gave him no choice. Had we trusted in something bigger than ourselves, the outcome might have been less . . . controversial."

"Or, maybe not," Dave surmised.

The silence extended for seconds.

"If you think I am the one who ought to apologize," Grant said, his voice somewhat hoarse as he defended himself, "you have another think coming. I'm not willing to leave the endowment fund here if we're going through some sort of political upheaval. And there will be upheaval if the homeless man continues to attend services. I can easily place the fund elsewhere, another church perhaps . . ."

Dave's mouth had gone tight with strain.

Mary Grace started to speak, but could not.

John thrust out his chin in a gesture of disapproval. He held out his hands, palms up. "We are *all* responsible for the well-being of the man who serves us. He has returned in faith and during Casey Boyd's service, he showed us his heart. I see no reason not to go ahead as planned and welcome him back with open arms."

Grant stammered, "But I don't think you are listening to what I have to say."

"If you leave, Grant, then you leave." There was no way John was going to let the man derail him. "God is calling people to his house. All people. And I aim to welcome them when they come. Unwashed. Unclean. Just like the rest of us."

"If you go, I believe Pastor Tibbits will regret it," Mary Grace said, startling herself. "He has respected you as a leader and loved you as a friend."

"I'm sorry it has to come to this," Grant said.

He left the room with no further sound.

CHAPTER TWENTY-SIX

The letter arrived in the mailbox, at Covenant Heights, stuck between the pages of a choir robe catalog. It lay beneath an electric bill and a stack of monthly newsletters, which had been returned for address updates.

Mary Grace didn't begin sifting through the mail until after 5:00 p.m. She put the bills into the treasurer's box, and piled the newsletters beside her computer to input the new information in the morning. She pitched the catalogue in the trashcan. They'd ordered choir robes recently because the choir had been growing. They wouldn't need new ones around Covenant Heights for a while.

But just before she got ready to switch off her computer and shut the lights off for the day, she lifted her mug and took a last sip of tea.

As she sipped, she happened to glance at the floor. Something caught her eye. An envelope had fallen beneath her desk. She picked it up and read the return address. *Hum. Nothing familiar.* Someone from Portland.

The envelope was long and cool in her hands, light blue with splotches of white woven in like linen fabric. It was addressed to Sam but, you know, these days that could mean anything. Mary Grace sliced it open with her official church letter opener, its pewter handle shaped like a cross.

She read the first line, and the second. She read the signature. She picked up the phone and called Sam at home.

"I think you'd better get over here. I know you're not officially back on staff yet, but I have something you need to see."

Sam held out his hand and Mary Grace put the letter in his hand. He examined the return address, the postmark, the pretty stamp with a picture of a boat. When he saw the handwriting on the envelope, he recognized it immediately. Aubrey's script had not changed since she'd been in her teens.

Dear Sam,

I think you already know how much it meant to me to see you again. I wasn't going to write and, if I get brave enough to mail this, you do not need to answer. I won't wait to hear from you. Hope it's okay I wrote you at your church. It was the only address I could find.

Gary came home from the treatment center last week. You should have seen the way the kids fussed over him. Billy wouldn't stop sitting in his lap and Hannah gave Elephant to him. Can you believe that? After all the money to ship that animal across two states, and she gives it away to her father first thing! He was trying to figure out how to give it back to her and then he looked at me. We were so in tune with each other, all I had to do was nod. He turned to Hannah and thanked her and said he would keep it always.

Children can be so much smarter than adults sometimes.

I am writing mostly to tell you that Gary made it home and to tell you "thank you" for praying for us. I know it's going to be a long road, but I feel like something beyond myself has given me the strength to carry on. I was walking into the bedroom last night because I was angry Gary had forgotten to give me a message from Channing's high school office and, all of a sudden, something else got hold of my mouth and I couldn't open it. All of a sudden, I knew what I was supposed to say. It came out just like that! Something I hadn't even been thinking. Gary, I said. I want you to know how proud I am of you. I want you to know that I admire the person you have worked to become over the past two months. I want you to know that I'm going to stand beside you and help that person become as strong as he can be. He said, I've been waiting to hear you say that ever since I got home.

Then he said, I just need to know you're standing beside me as an equal, Aubrey. I don't need you to help me become stronger. I'm the one responsible for that. I'm not going to be a husband who takes from you and doesn't give back. I'm finished with living my life like that.

Until then, *I* didn't know how badly I needed to hear *that*.

Someday, I may tell Gary about our time together. Or, I may not. I'm going to pray about that, too. I just wanted you to know how much I cherished seeing you, Sam. Being in the seaside cottage changed my life. I am convinced this turn of events with my husband would never have happened if you had not showed me the way to your Father's heart.

I will never forget you, Sam. I will think of you often. I will remember you well.

As always,
Aubrey

CHAPTER TWENTY-SEVEN

Sam's call to pastor had been a moment, he would still insist years later, that was much easier *felt* than talked about. As he stood on the ladder at his sister's house, craning his neck so he could paint a second coat on the trim over the garage door, Sam might as well have been that college student again, lying in the rusty dorm bed, craning his neck to stare at the bricks in the ceiling. Trying to breathe. Remembering the words he'd once heard in his spirit.

You have been chosen by me to feed the ones I love.

That night so long ago, he hadn't been able to sleep. He'd leapt out of bed and turned on his light and his roommate had moaned, "Sam, what are you doing? Can't it wait until morning?"

"No," he'd insisted. And he'd gone digging through his closet, throwing everything frantically out of the way, his shoes landing in hollow thumps behind him, his high school yearbook coming to rest with its pages splayed like wings, the tangle of dirty clothes ending up in a knot in the middle of the room. Then he had it in his hand—the blue-leather book inscribed with his name in small gold letters: SAMUEL JAMES TIBBITS.

The cover was peeling off the Bible because he had once carried it with him to read in the sand. A church bulletin fell out and he saw the date of the last time he'd played Hangman with a friend in the pew. *Amazing, that he could have taken any of this so lightly!*

He began thumbing through, trying to find the Scripture. *Him.* Sam Tibbits. Who never got stickers in third-grade Sunday school because he couldn't remember to return his memory verses to class. He guessed that, probably, when he found the page he was searching for, it wouldn't mean anything. But he was wrong. When he found it, he stared at the page. He read the words over and over again.

And go to the land that I will show you.

Reading that Scripture so long ago, something inside Sam Tibbits had soared. The words seemed to lift and move and glimmer on the page. They became alive and personal and enfolded themselves around his questioning heart.

Those had been the days he'd spent living on hope, feeling both afraid and inadequate, believing his heavenly Father to prepare the way before him, swept along by a glorious current, something beyond himself.

He understood so much about himself now, because the Father had showed him firsthand.

Those who have left their first love behind would do well to consider. Where is the blessedness they once spoke of?

"Thank you, Father. Oh, thank you for not giving up on me," Sam whispered as he wielded the paintbrush high overhead.

What, then, is healing if you have no intention of going to visit the sick? Why do you need love if you're going to distance yourself? What is a gift from the

Lord if you're going to hoard it for yourself and not give it away again?

He had arrived once more at Covenant Heights. The land which his Father had shown him. Oh, how good it felt to be certain again!

Sam stands at the edge of a path, enjoying the maple leaves. They sift slowly from black branches above his head. The sky is so blue it makes his head throb.

The heat has cured the grass until it's the same color as Ginny's fur. The dog is skittish today. When she steps into heaps of maple leaves, they crackle beneath her feet. She doesn't remember that she loved playing in them last year. She hops sideways in distress and Sam laughs at her for forgetting what each new season will bring.

Another three months and, crazy dog, she'll have to remember snow.

Sam didn't expect so many Covenant Heights church members to drive this far for the antique car rally in deep Iowa farm country. Exploring the countryside is something he's never taken the time to do for himself before. The autumn sun bathes the curves of the old automobiles in a gold wash of light. Everywhere he turns, he sees someone he knows.

He and Mary Grace sit on the grass eating ice cream from the old creamery, and John McKinley catches him with a mouthful of banana walnut. "Good to have you back at the helm, Sam." John pats him heartily on the back.

When they browse in the Old World Lace Shop, Dottie Graham waves from across the aisle, her eyes darting from Mary Grace to him, and from him to Mary Grace again. She holds up a doily and (as if it would block any noise at all!) stage whispers behind it, "Well, isn't this just the nicest thing?" to her friend.

Hunter, of course, is fascinated by the cars. Most of them are polished to perfection, the gleam coming off their fenders enough to signal someone stranded on another hill. The signs in their windows say DO NOT TOUCH. But there is a Cadillac convertible from the 1960s with a black and white paint job and red leather interior that doesn't have a sign. Hunter has been inside that car three times.

Sam hasn't heard from Aubrey again since her letter, and he knows he never will. She will always be a part of him because loving her helped make him who he is. She taught him to dig for clams. She taught him that there are parts of human love, too, that never end. That love doesn't always die and that, sometimes, love becomes stronger when it changes.

Sometime when the wind kicks up and the cool breeze floods across the Iowa hills, something about it makes him imagine the smell of salt air. He'll glance up and see a gull. He imagines he can hear the sea.

He thinks of Aubrey then.

He knows he won't go back. He will go forward, press closer, to his own life instead.

Sam does not often ask Mary Grace what she thinks of them as a couple. It has been easy to keep their new friendship quiet through the heated end of summer, because he has been on leave. Once he takes over his office again, first thing Tuesday morning, he knows everyone will give him advice like family. He and Mary Grace will both have plenty of opinions coming their way.

Sam has taken too long dreaming by the maples. He hears Mary Grace calling his name. She is at the furniture exhibit, standing beside an enormous handmade chair.

A cotton candy stand grabs his attention. He fumbles with Ginny's leash as he tries to get the change in his pocket. Even though Mary Grace is waving her hands, mouthing no, no, he buys her a bouquet of it anyway. Not just one puff of cotton candy for his girl— absolutely unthinkable! They have orange. And pink. And blue. That is something new these days. She must have all the colors. He loves that about Mary Grace. She is brilliant color, all the time. How could he have missed it all these years?

Sam sometimes catches a look in her eye when the two of them are together, a glimmer that seems to reflect his soul. He knows to pray, to seek the Lord's face about what he might be feeling. Today, very cautiously, he asks Mary Grace: "How would you feel if we began to think of our future?" He could also say, "Because I am finished thinking about my past." But he doesn't.

She laughs. "Only if you'll let me clean out your freezer." She props her hands on her hips like a truant officer, her fingernails flashing orange, her smile illuminating his day. "I've never seen so many casserole dishes with phone numbers in all my life. From now on, no one puts casseroles in your freezer but me."

Sam laughs too, wraps his arm around her and draws her against him. He knows now, in God's plan, she will be the one.

Overhead, the clouds always drift westward. Very soon, they will rise over the mountains. Eventually, they will sail forth over the sea.

Dearest Reader,

What joy it has been to write this book for you! I'm scribbling this letter while the book is still four days from completion, knowing that the Father will be faithful to provide the ending that will touch your hearts for Him. I set out to write a book about a universal story. What would happen if we happened upon an old love? How would we respond? What would we say? And would we be able to walk away satisfied without wishing to regain our pasts?

No two writers work the same. I begin with a character and, with a lot of prayer, let that character guide me. As Sam Tibbits struggled as a pastor in *Remember Me*, his journey taught me so much about my own views of people. It is easy to name the idols that we often live by in our lives. Our careers. Our time. Our appearances. Our belongings. Our plans. But never before had I thought of *people* being idols.

As I began to understand that Sam had placed Aubrey above God in his life, it became apparent that (1) the Father brought these two back together so Sam could offer Christ's healing hope to her; and (2) the Father wanted Sam to see the truth about his own life. How often I do the same thing that Sam does! It is so easy to look to *people* to fill the emptiness that only the Father can fill.

Tinsley Spessard is a beautiful young mother who

authored the discussion questions in *Remember Me*. Tinsley and I are in a women's covenant group together. When the time came to submit these questions, I was too close to Sam and Aubrey's lives to step away and be able to see clearly. Tinsley volunteered to read the book and see what questions the Father would put on her heart. I think you'll agree that God moved through her in a powerful direction. Blessings on you and your study group as you consider the questions Tinsley poses. Her thoughts bring me so much joy! Oh, how I'd like to be a fly on the wall and listen to your insights, too.

Know that I'm praying for you and your journey with the Father, especially as I'm writing these final pages. My dear one, may your every breath be filled with prayer to the Father to guide you. May your every struggle end with new, personal insight of His providence and plan. May you always return to Jesus, because His love is always first love!

Deborah Bedford
www.deborahbedfordbooks.com
Box 9175
Jackson Hole, WY 83001

Center Point Publishing

600 Brooks Road ● PO Box 1
Thorndike ME 04986-0001 USA

(207) 568-3717

US & Canada:
1 800 929-9108